Caught In The Loop

By L.S. Anderson

Hot Iron Press
Phoenix

Manufactured in the United States of America. This edition published by Hot Iron Press. To order, send $14.95 per copy ($12.95 + $2 postage and handling) to Hot Iron Press, 207 W. Clarendon #14H, Phoenix, AZ 85013-3416. Additional inquiries? Call (602) 277-3464.

10 9 8 7 6 5 4 3 2 1

Library of Congress Catalog Card Number: 92-90362

Publisher's Cataloging in Publication Data
Anderson, L.S.
    Caught in the loop
    1. Cattle Ranching.   2. Western Fiction.
    3. Humor—Western.   I. Title.
              1992   813'.54

ISBN 0-9633672-1-8

Caught In The Loop produced by Mary Westheimer, Via Writing & Publishing Services

Cover by Mark Woodruff

Contents

Preface

This historically-based chronicle of cattle ranching business in Arizona is about old-timers who had to make a living off the land and newcomers who came to enjoy it with little regard for the economics of the business.

What happens to the people in this story surprises old-timers and newcomers alike.

Acknowledgments

Family and friends meld East and West.
Each made a unique contribution to this book.
All are caught in the loop of my thanks.

The First Families
of Arizona
The Phoenix
Museum of History
John Anderson
Joe Anderson
Alexandra Anderson
Candace Anderson
Carolyn A. Lee

Shirley Arnstein
Ben Avery
Irene Benedict
Joel Benedict
Evadna Burba

Dorothy Byrd
Willownet Cable
Mary Caress
Marilyn Click
Merilyn Davis
Angeline Dent
Dr. Duke Dent
Alice Graham
Marie Forsyth
Alfarata Hansel
Dr. Grace Kaiser
Irene Kyle
Warren Kyle
Dorothy Lykes
Helen Lawler

Frances Libby
Ruth Magadini
Rosalyn Mandel
Marguerite Noble
Florence Priest
Polly Rosenbaum
Nadine Smith
Bob Stafford
Sue Stafford
Bonnie Tomeoni
Leroy Tucker
Velma Tucker
Mary Ann Turner
Irys Woodford
John Woodford

With appreciation and commendation for the people of the
Western cattle ranch industry. They inspire me and enrich my
life, and I am proud to be one of them.

Introduction

Before the West was tamed, the wide open spaces were enjoyed by a few hardy souls. The first competitors for open land were cattlemen, mineral prospectors and farmers. This contest continued with only piecemeal regulation for about a century. Congress first recognized the rights of mining claims, then homesteads, next timber, followed by grazing, parks and recreation. In spite of on-going efforts, law makers found it impossible to make everybody happy. Fighting Indians, feuding homesteaders and squabbling squatters continued to kick up dust.

To mark territory and confine livestock, cattle ranchers put up barbed-wire fences. Now they were in a position to control numbers grazed and to conserve land for long-term use.

When cattle ranching became unprofitable for some cattlemen, they sold their outfits to men who didn't need to make money—they already had it. These new ranch owners were able to hire physical work done by local folk or former owners. When they competed with each other, economic reasoning wasn't part of the deal.

Today, raisers of livestock continue to improve ranches by better management. They agree with the idea of multiple use of public land—even though they are roped and tied by economic and political restraints.

People with other interests push and pull from all directions. Loud cries come from off-road vehicle owners, recreational players, energy developers, wildlife protectors, timber harvesters, wilderness environmentalists, and wild horse and burro preservers.

"Move over, Eastern dude."

"Get lost, Western cowboy."

An Eastern Dude Looms On The Horizon

With the cadence of a Western ballad, the word "West" kept time with Elwin Luscomb's beating heart. The drumming in his forty-five-year-old chest picked up speed during the elevator ride in a highrise building in downtown Tucson.

Willing his tall, well-knit frame to slow down, he paused at office door number 43. His name headed the list of four lawyers.

Inside, the receptionist broke the silence when she slid back from her desk. "Mr. Lussss...comb? I'll ring. They're expecting you."

Three men entered the room.

Arms crossed, chin raised, Elwin waited for compliments.

Law-firm partners vied for attention. Their voices

rose, sounds and words overlapping. "My God, El-win!...Wild West show?...you going?...Mardi Gras in Arizona?...not *you*...for Halloween!...wearing high-heeled boots and a ten-gallon hat? ...don't believe what I'm seeing...why the getup?"

Elwin flashed a gap-toothed smile. "I'm leaving for my spread right after our meeting."

One of the partners gulped. "Again? You bought that ranch two weeks ago and you've hardly been in the office since."

"I know."

After several seconds Elwin turned from looking out the window at the Santa Catalina Mountains and let his gaze sweep over the walls hung with Western art. Whenever he looked at the paintings, he felt part of the pictures by Remington, Russell and other artists. Every time he viewed *Riders of the Open Range* he smelled sage, heard thundering hooves, and felt leather between fingers and seat.

Settling Stetson on wavy brown hair, Elwin said, "I can feel the crispness of fresh air and hear the 'Git along, little dogies,' now that I own a ranch. I am one of *them.*"

One of the partners asked, "In your *dude* outfit?"

Elwin straightened his bola tie, manicured fingertips lingering on smooth turquoise stone. "Harumph. Well, after a hundred years, some upgrading is expected in clothing, but the spirit of those days is alive today."

He slapped both palms on the desk top and looked each partner in the eye. "I intend to embrace values and live by the code of The Old West."

Dude Arrival

Pete Moore's shouts crackled through the thick underbrush, as the old cowman rode horseback toward his son. "The whole Southwest is going to the damn dudes!"

Young Fred Moore, approaching from a sandy bank of the San Pedro River, bent his lithe body forward in the saddle and greeted his father. "Hi, Dad, it's good to be home. I know why you're riled up and yelling. Mom told me the Luscombs bought the Johnson Place."

"Yeah, the Eastern visitors beat me out of it."

The two men turned their horses from the river and rode through the brush, across the dirt road and up into foothills of towering South Mountain.

Stopping atop the first bare knoll, Pete leaned over the saddle horn and fanned his wrinkled face with his cowboy hat. "There it is," he said, pointing to a strip of irrigated land along the river bank. "The Old Johnson Place. I've been working and dickering to buy that ranch for years. It joins us and would make a dandy

11

line camp and holding pasture, or a separate little outfit." Under his breath he added, "For you."

Fred reined to face his father. "You and Buzzard Ben are long-time friends. Maybe if you two hadn't tried to outmaneuver each other, a third party couldn't have moved in."

Pete reached into his shirt pocket for cigarette makings. "Luscomb was the lawyer in the deal," he said self-righteously. "Who would ever have thought a dude would want that place for himself. It's a long haul from Tucson with headquarters on the wrong side of the river. There's no other Easterners for neighbors, and during flood time they'll be as marooned as rats on an island. Good Lord, I never figured Luscomb to buy the Old Johnson Place."

"But he did."

"Yes, and he'll ruin it, if we can't get him to leave."

"Did you try to buy him out?"

"Hell yes, but he wouldn't sell. Says he wants to be a cattleman. When I get through with him, he'll go back where he came from."

"Now, Dad, it's not like you to make threats."

"Don't worry. It'll be legal. Luscomb's a lawyer. I've an idea he'll know when he's beat. Leave the Easterners to me, son. They're my personal problem. It's up to you to stay in school and learn to be a combination bookkeeper and engineer. That's what it takes to be a cattleman these days."

Fred ran slender fingers through short brown hair and resettled his broad-brimmed hat. "I hope you won't start feuding with Buzzard Ben. You two old-timers are friends and neighbors. Can't you trust him?"

"Hell no! I wouldn't trust that jug-headed, long-beaked rascal any farther than I could throw a bull by the tail." He took a long drag on his smoke, sobered and added, "But I'd a damn sight rather he'd bought that ranch than the dudes. At least he'd leave it alone and I could buy it for a fair price in a few years." He spoke through clenched store-bought teeth. "I have to get it away from Luscomb before he puts a fancy house and a bunch of unusable corrals on the land."

Fred looked past the Old Johnson Place, over to Saddle Mountain, down the other side of the river, and back across the lower crossing to his own home. "Not much water in the San Pedro for summer," he commented, surveying the half-mile-wide sandy bed with a mere trickle winding down the center. "This country is as hot and dry as I can remember."

"Sure is," admitted Pete, tugging a Stetson lower on his bald head. "You wouldn't think a dude would want to buy a ranch on this godforsaken, droughty, poor, mountainous desert range, would you?"

"Don't try to convince me. Save that talk for Elwin and Gladys Luscomb. By the way," he asked, looking down on three adobe shacks, barbed-wire-fenced pastures, and sixty-acre strip of land along the river. "When do they take possession?"

"Not take, took! They moved in last week like a couple of squatters expecting to stay forever."

Fred reined his horse off the knoll. "They might do exactly that." Over his shoulder he called, "Give them a chance, Dad. They may be nice people."

Pete followed horseback, talking heatedly. "I wouldn't mind if they were content to move into a little house and be nice people. They are going into the cow business. Can you imagine that gap-toothed lawyer raising stock? Why, I've fired skim-milk cowboys that had forgot more than Luscomb will ever learn. He may be smart in the courtroom, but he doesn't know his ass from a hot rock when it comes to working cattle. He'll probably buy a big white horse and gallop hell-for-leather over the countryside and run more fat off our cows in one mad dash than they can gain back in six weeks of slim pickings off this brush-covered range. Hey! Where are you headed?"

"I saw a line-backed cow we missed when I was home on school break. I'll circle and cut her off from the mesquites."

Pete stopped his tirade and spoke to himself. "He's a natural cowboy. He can spot an animal a mile away and knows what moves it'll probably make. Whoever heard of dudes out-thinking a cow?" He spurred his horse lightly. "I won't let them out-think me either."

An hour later, Pete and Fred saw a man riding hard, chasing a large red steer. Pete turned to his son. "It's Buzzard Ben. Drive this cow home. Gate is open at the first corral. You've got clear ground from here on. I'll see what's got into Ben. He doesn't run cattle just to be running them. I never saw that steer before."

Fred nodded and rode south.

"Look out!" yelled the cowboy, as he chased the steer across the riverbed. Pete reined his horse out of the way.

When the animal stumbled up the trail and disappeared into a brush thicket, the two men turned their mounts back toward the river.

"That animal," said Buzzard Ben, motioning with his thumb and looking down his long nose, "is a steer belonging to your Eastern friend."

Pete's hackles rose. "Luscomb didn't buy that steer with the place. I know the cattle he bought."

Ben bared his head to blazing sun, raked his forearm across scraggly hair and sneered. "Hey, let me tell you about the new deal. Your smart lawyer pal has put a

14

hundred extra big steers on the range. I said *big* steers."
He slammed his hat on his head so hard, hair stuck
out over bat-winged ears. "And by god, they'll not locate on my land. I'll chase every one back across the
San Pedro River as soon as he sets a foot on my side."

"Now wait a damn minute. Luscomb's not my Eastern
friend, and what's more, he's not my smart lawyer pal.
If it was legal I'd chase that damn dude and his cattle
to hell personally."

Buzzard Ben pounded the pommel of his saddle. "If
you hadn't hired that smart-assed lawyer to beat me
out, I'da bought the Old Johnson Place."

Pete raised his wrinkled chin and thrust it forward.
"If you hadn't been so damned set on getting hold of
more country, I'd have bought it. Don't forget, my
spring waters that land along the river."

The two men faced each other. Necks forward,
spurs back, each waited for the other to move first.

In the saddle, Pete seemed larger than the five-feet-
seven inches he claimed to be. Although his
movements were youthful, his wrinkled, sun-weath-
ered face made him look older than his fifty-eight years.

Ben, a lanky bachelor in his late forties, was the
prototype of a good-looking cowboy. Thick eyebrows
arched over devilish brown eyes, and laugh-lines
formed parentheses around pursed lips.

Tension broke when a high-pitched feminine voice
called out, "Yoo-hoo, oh, yoo-hoo."

Both men turned to see a handsome red-haired
woman, wearing a shrimp-colored Western shirt and
Levi's. She rode a black horse across the wide riverbed
and small stream.

"It's Gladys Luscomb," whispered Pete.

"Let's get her," said Ben, spurring his mount.

"Wait," called Pete. "You can't chase her home the

way you did that steer."

"Who says I can't? It's open season on dudes."

The three riders met. Mrs. Luscomb trilled, "Maybe I should say 'howdy partner'." She reared her black horse to a sudden stop.

Pete rode between Ben and Mrs. Luscomb. Touching thumb and finger tip to his wide-brimmed hat, he said swiftly, "Yes, ma'am, but we're after a calf and can't stop. Be seeing you." He nudged Ben's horse from behind, but Ben wasn't budging. He was staring open-mouthed at Mrs. Luscomb.

Gladys tossed her bright red hair. "I saw you gallop after one of our new steers," she said to Ben. "I thought it was simply beautiful riding. Of course," she added demurely, "I've heard one thing you can expect from the West is helpful neighbors."

Buzzard Ben didn't seem to be able to take his eyes off the bulging front of Mrs. Luscomb's shirt.

"Goodbye, ma'am," said Pete. Turning, he kicked one foot free of the stirrup and raked a spur across the rump of Ben's horse. The cowboy grabbed his reins and hat as his mount jumped. The two men loped down river, leaving the well-padded female astride her black horse.

Pete's wrinkled face was near the color of the blazing sun. "That woman is a dude!" he yelled. "She's married to a dude, and I understand she's got a grown dude daughter."

Ben had the look of a man who has been hit over the head with a branding iron. "Man," he breathed. "She puts a Holstein cow to shame. Did you ever see a woman with such tits? I'll wager she's not a day over forty-five, and she sits a horse real fine."

Pete slowed his horse. "I thought you were with me. Don't you want to get rid of the Luscombs?"

16

Ben pulled on his reins and blinked his veiled eyes. "Elwin? Sure. I'll help on the husband. Shall we shoot him, trap him, or use poison bait?"

"Why, you ornery rascal. I told Fred I can't trust you any farther than I can throw a bull by the tail. If I get rid of the Luscombs I'll have to do it alone. That's for damn sure."

After Pete left his neighbor, he rode up river to his own headquarters. He noted with satisfaction his son had put the cow on green pasture.

It was mid-afternoon when Pete left his horse at the corral and walked to his house, an old adobe with a corrugated iron roof and wooden, screened front porch. He mumbled, "If Luscomb stays on the Old Johnson Place long enough to do any improvement, he'll probably build corrals to hell and gone from his front door. Any dude outfit I ever saw had corrals so far from the house a man had to keep a horse saddled to ride back and forth."

He paused at the hydrant at a porch corner and sloshed water on hands and ruddy face. Removing his spurs but still wearing a Stetson pushed back on his forehead, he stepped into the kitchen.

A slender, brown-skinned woman, with salt-and-pepper hair hanging down her back, was frying steak at a wood stove. "Fred told me you'd be along."

Pete hung his hat on a wall peg. When he looked at his wife, he smiled. "This is when I think a woman is prettiest—bending over the kitchen stove."

Pearl laughed. The tone was low-pitched and musical. "What put your mind on that track? You're not usually so hungry mid-afternoon."

"I met Buzzard Ben at the Johnson river crossing—also that full-blown wife of Elwin's."

His wife lifted a stove lid to pour grease into the

fire. Her high cheekbones, highlighted by the open flame, looked like burnished copper. "Somebody ought to warn Mrs. Luscomb about Buzzard Ben. He's a lone wolf and howls like one."

"From what I've seen of that redhead," answered Pete, pulling up to the table, "she'll take care of herself." He heaped his plate with chili beans and fried beef. Heat of the food, both from fire and pepper, easily outdid the heat of the day.

Grasping a fork in his tobacco-stained hand, Pete looked at his wife. "Pearl, that Eastern dude doesn't know we wait for a rainy season to grow extra feed before we put more cattle on the open range in this spring country."

"He'll learn."

"Fred say where he was going?"

"Town."

"He's only been home from a session of summer school half a day...probably took the Ford. What is there about a ten-mile ride over a dirt road to the bright lights of a little copper mining town that draws the boys?"

"Same thing used to draw you," reminded the slender woman pouring black coffee into white enamelware cups.

Pete sighed and let his mind slip back for a few satisfied moments to his own courting days, before he jerked himself to the present. "I believe I'll sashay up to the river crossing tomorrow and have another talk with Luscombs. Maybe I can get them to leave before it's too late."

"The Old Johnson Place is sold. It's not like you to butt your head against a wall."

Pete jabbed his fork into a piece of meat. "As far as I'm concerned, the sale is not final. I'll know when the matter is settled for good, because I'll do the settling."

Digging Up The Past

Pete didn't go to Luscombs' next day as planned. He and Fred drove to the far end of the ranch where they poured hot asphalt into the bottom of a leaky water tank. They spent two days hunting a sick calf. Then they had to pull the sucker rod out of the well at headquarters and put on new leathers. Work went on.

A week later the Moores saddled up their horses and rode up river and across to Luscombs'. "Sunup," said Pete. "The dudes will be asleep." He chuckled. "This is almost like sneaking up on them. Now, soon as they get the sand out of their eyes, you buttonhole Gladys. Keep her talking so I can have a man-to-man talk with Elwin. When ladies are around, I spend so much time watching my language I can't keep my mind on what I'm saying."

"You want me to just talk with the redhead?"

Pete glowered. "It's bad enough to watch Buzzard Ben following that dude woman around like a stud horse in May without having you get ideas."

Fred laughed. "She's female all the way, Dad." He

gave a long, low whistle.

"The thought of you so much as looking at a dude woman...." Pete's voice sputtered out as the two men rode their horses around the last turn in the road and approached the Old Johnson Place. At the side of the ramshackle adobe house three Mexican boys, handkerchiefs tied around their heads, shovelled wet dirt over and over in a shallow hole. In the middle of the front yard Gladys Luscomb, wearing short shorts and red halter, peered through a level pointed in the direction of a tractor across the yard.

Buzzard Ben, perched on the crawler-type seat, waited for her come-on sign.

In a few seconds she waved. Ben started the machine. When it plunged forward, his hat flew off. He sat frozen at the controls.

Pete pulled on his reins and yelled, "God Almighty, what's going on?"

As the machine roared ahead, Pete and Fred galloped their horses forward. Both men yelled, "Ben! The clutch! Brake! Left hand, Ben...your left hand!"

It was impossible for the old cowboy to hear instructions over the roar of the powerful motor. However, he must have stepped on the brake and released the clutch on the same side. The tractor spun in a tight circle, the bulldozer in front scooping up dirt and rocks.

Gladys was still bent over peering into the telescope mounted atop a tripod. She moved the instrument back and forth, around and around in a futile attempt to find the tractor in the glass.

Ben, after two full spins, made another grab for the controls. The whirling machine stopped, lurched and bucked toward Gladys.

Pete and Fred, whose horses had backed away from

the tractor, turned and galloped forward again.

"My God!" yelled Pete. "Ben's no tractor driver. Locoed fool will push the mound of dirt right over the tripod, redhead and all."

Gladys straightened, gave one horrified look, screamed and ran. The mound of dirt grew in front of the tractor as the tracks moved steadily and inexorably, the 'dozer pushing the levelling instrument to one side and shoving on toward the house.

Ben threw a helpless look over his shoulder. He made a move to jump, then slumped in the seat and covered his head with both arms.

The bulldozer blade caught the center post of the house. The post buckled but held, as the mound of dirt spilled onto the open porch. When the overloaded bulldozer put so much strain on the tractor engine, it roared the death rattle and died.

Emotion fogging his voice, Pete demanded, "Ben, you damned old fool, what are you doing?"

Ben slid off the seat, stumbled along the ground, and yanked on both earlobes. "I don't know, but I sure done it."

Three Mexican boys, shovels in hand, joined the group.

Gladys leaned against the corner post. "What a horrible, horrible mess. I only wanted the yard smooth for a lawn." She bent her head and sobbed.

The tractor had taken a six-foot swath, five inches deep and one hundred and fifty feet long—a zigzag path with two swirls—in the center of the yard.

Ben said, "Well, it'll make you a real good path. All sunk nice. Wide too."

The Mexican boys began talking in Spanish.

Gladys laid her head on her bare arms and sobbed louder.

21

Young Fred climbed onto the tractor seat, started the engine and managed to back the machine into the yard.

Ben collapsed on the dirt pile. Shock had apparently caught up with him.

Pete, looking around, mumbled, "Looks like I'm left to comfort the redhead." Stepping close, he gave Gladys tentative pats on her bare back. What was it about a woman crying.... He pulled his rough old hand away and said, "There, there, ma'am, you go in the house and lay down. We'll clean up the porch."

"I can't get in," she wailed.

"That's one good thing about these ranch houses," said Pete philosophically, "there's lots of doors."

Ben, spurs jingling, walked to the middle of the yard and picked up his grimy felt hat. Hurrying back to the porch, beating the dusty Stetson against his thigh at every step, he shouldered his way up to Pete as through comforting the redhead was his chore.

"Where's your husband?" asked Pete.

"Elwin went to Tucson to order an electric plant. He told me not to start this job, but I was...." She broke into fresh sobs.

Pete glowered at Ben. "You ought to have to scoop up this dirt and spread it back on the yard with your bare hands."

"Don't you go givin' me orders, Pete Moore," shouted the cowboy, his long nose close to Pete's wrinkled face.

Gladys stopped sobbing and asked, "Will somebody see if the level is broken?"

Quick to oblige, Ben stepped forward. Soft dirt spilled over the tops of his boots, as he tugged at the legs of the half-buried tripod. The three Mexican boys started shovelling dirt off the porch, while Pete and

Fred went down to the irrigating ditch a hundred feet behind the house and sat on the ground under a cottonwood tree. After pouring sand from his boots Ben hobbled after them. He walked carefully to avoid stepping on cockleburs.

A quarter of an hour later Gladys, wearing fresh make-up, followed the men to the ditch bank.

"You know, Mrs. Luscomb," said Fred, "I believe you will get along better if you lay out your yard and put up your markers before you try to use the tractor."

Gladys took a hitch in her halter and sat cross-legged. "That's what I mean about Western people being so neighborly. Honestly, I can't get over it."

Pete snorted. "The road to Tucson is mostly dirt. Did Elwin figure on coming back before dark?"

"This afternoon. He didn't have much to do and he drives very fast." Gladys furrowed her white brow and seemed ready to break into tears again. "I wanted to surprise Elwin by leveling the yard so that we could get right to work on the house."

At the word 'house', Pete's mind conjured up a picture of a two-story mansion with bay windows, railings, balconies, fancy grillwork, and lots of gingerbread. He asked, "Are you planning to build your new house right next to the old one?" It was as close to a personal question as Pete dared go.

"Why, Mr. Moore," Gladys answered, "we're not planning to build a new house."

Wonder showing on his face, Pete glanced at Fred. He pointed to the weathered adobe shack with rusty corrugated iron roof and unscreened windows. "You're not going to live there?"

Gladys clapped her hands. "I didn't know you were so interested. That's why I hired those laborers over there," she said, pointing to the Mexican boys, who

23

were still cleaning dirt off the porch. "Elwin and I plan to restore the house, though of course we'll add modern conveniences." A quick frown creased her smooth forehead, as she glanced from one man's blank face to another. "Don't you think it is a shame the way the Old West is dying? Honestly!" Her laugh tinkled. "I suppose you natives don't appreciate your glorious heritage—the wild, romantic West."

Buzzard Ben, his feet soaking in the irrigating ditch, looked sullen but did not respond.

"Now, ma'am," said Pete, "we like it here better than anybody. We think the West is growing and progressing, slow but sure. Only last week I was explaining...wasn't I Fred?" He turned toward his son.

Gladys rose to her feet in one graceful movement and started back to the house. "Come, let's all have cold lemonade. I'll show you our blueprints."

Pete was a little happier knowing the dudes weren't going to up the price of the Old Johnson Place by building an expensive mansion on it. He and Fred followed Mrs. Luscomb.

As soon as they started walking, Ben pulled his feet from the ditch and struggled to pull on his boots. Looking back, Pete grinned at the cowboy's obvious discomfort. "Dry those wet feet on your shirttail, you old buzzard, and you'll have better luck getting your boots back on."

In the kitchen Mrs. Luscomb served the men cups of lemonade from a thermos jug. Ben arrived during the second round. From a cabinet inside the back door, Gladys brought out several rolls of blue-colored paper and passed one to Pete. "Our plans," she said.

Pete spread the roll with this thumbs and peered helplessly at the white lines before passing the roll to his son. Gladys handed three more rolls to Fred and said, "Maybe you'll understand better if I show you. Right here," she said, stepping out of the kitchen and into the wide hall, "at this very spot," pointing to the splintered wooden floor, "was an old well."

"Yeah," said Ben, unimpressed. "I remember that old well. Me and Pete here was kids when we pulled old man Johnson out of there early one morning lookin' like a drowned rat."

Remembering, Pete added, "Then we helped him fill it in—the whole twenty feet—with a shovel. We boarded it over, too." He explained to Gladys, "No need for a well between two rooms of an adobe house after you got piped water to the corner outside. There was some sense to having a well right here when Indians were attacking."

"That's just what I mean," said Gladys, taking the blueprints from Fred. "Imagine, filling in a romantic old well."

Buzzard Ben moved close to Gladys. "Old man Johnson didn't think it was so all-fired romantic. It was wintertime when he fell in, and cold water like to froze him 'fore it almost drowned him. When we pulled him out, he was stiff as a cactus and cold as a snake's belly in the middle of January."

Gladys, backing away from Ben, said, "And we understand this hallway was formerly open between the two main rooms and used to house the wagon for safety during raids by marauding Apache Indians."

Ben said, "You ain't aimin' to drive your car in here?"

"Oh, my no. We're going to use this for a breezeway."

"Step outside," said Pete, "and get breeze most anytime."

Gladys gazed overhead at weathered plasterboard. "We'll reline the ceiling and paint it sky blue."

"We always figured a roof was to keep the sky out,"

said Pete, wondering if Mrs. Luscomb might be taking too many liberties with Johnson's old house.

Turning toward the kitchen, Fred asked, "Shall I bring more lemonade?"

Gladys smiled, nodded, and stepped into the large front room. Waving rolls of blueprint, she spoke with enthusiasm.

"Naturally, we'll do most of our entertaining in this area."

"Entertaining?" asked Pete, thinking in terms of the wild dances at the barn next to an abandoned schoolhouse near his headquarters.

"Yes, indeed," Gladys answered. "The minute we finish, we're having Open House. We plan to go completely native."

She took half a dozen steps. "At this door we'll add a master bedroom." She opened one roll and spread the blue paper on a card table. "See? Our most difficult problem was the addition of bathrooms. The half bath at the kitchen entrance was easy enough, but..."

"Half-bath?" inquired Ben, pulling at his long nose. "Which half?"

Gladys left her sentence unfinished and didn't answer.

Fred joined the trio. "How about your furnishings and color scheme?"

"Wild, bold colors—the primitive, you know." She pointed. "There will be raffia rugs, Venetian blinds, rattan furniture, all with Indian and Mexican overtones. I'm having my personal things shipped from the East. I collect bone china," she finished modestly. "It should be here any day."

"Well," said Ben, pointing out an open window, "you can get all the bones you want right here. Lots of Injun fightin' hereabouts in the olden days, and plenty of buryin' places."

Gladys dropped the blueprints and spun around.

With placating tones Ben added, "Don't worry. Never was no ghosts, an' old man Johnson did the best he could to cover up that grave in the yard."

With a cry of delight Mrs. Luscomb ran out to a spot between the house and corrals. "Here?" she asked, digging red fingernails into the bare, rocky ground.

The men standing nearby nodded. Ben, seemingly happy to have gained Mrs. Luscomb's attention and approval, moved close and helped her dig.

She backed away, straightened and said, "Honestly, the way you Westerners fail to appreciate what's under your noses. This is an archaeologist's dream."

"It sure was a nightmare to old man Johnson," said Ben. "Somebody was always diggin' around in the yard. Kept him busy throwin' in all his wire and tin cans to keep it covered up."

Gladys glanced meaningfully from Fred to the dirt in her hands, shrugged prettily and with lifted eyebrows and pleading tones asked, "Perhaps the tractor?"

"Sure," agreed Fred. He seemed relieved to have a chance for some action. Grinning, he climbed onto the yellow tractor and settled into the padded seat.

Disgusted, Pete walked off with Ben. "If I didn't need to talk with Elwin Luscomb, I'd leave," he said. "That boy of mine has work to do at home. We have a cement water trough to build, and look at him—digging up ancient history for a dude woman."

"Yeah," said Ben, turning back to the action, "me too."

Pete tied his horse in the shade of a mesquite bush and sat down to wait. It was a long and miserable vigil. He felt sweat dampening the back of his shirt and oozing from under armpits. In spite of discomfort, he left his chaps on.

Late afternoon Elwin Luscomb drove up in a big

green sedan. Recklessly, he spun automobile wheels over a spot in the fence where barbed wires lay on the ground and stopped the car in a swirl of dust near the mound of dirt Mexican boys had moved off the porch.

"I say," he called. "What's going on here?" Polished cowboy boots hit the dust, as the tall man slid out of his car.

Young Fred, eyes on his work and ears filled with the roar of the motor, kept bulldozing wire and old cans over the side yard.

"We started to level," called Gladys to her husband, confusing the events of the morning, "and guess what we bought?"

Elwin, long legs spread wide, stood like an angry policeman waiting for an explanation.

Gladys shouted, "It's an Indian ruin!"

"That," scoffed Elwin, watching Fred back up, jerk ahead and send another load of old cans rolling and wire tangling, "is a pile of refuse."

"Not underneath," insisted Gladys, appealing to Ben and Fred for verification.

"Yep," agreed the old cowboy, "a burial mound—the place is full of 'em."

"Well, now, this is a find," said Elwin, baring his teeth in a surprised gap-tooth smile. "Right in our yard, eh? I assumed we might pick up an arrowhead around— this being Apache country—but a real burial spot?" He turned quickly on polished boot heels. "We'd better have a drink to celebrate."

His cowboy outfit was summer weight, tailored to fit, Panama hat, Western style. He threw open the car trunk. Pete peered inside, glancing with curiosity and the rows of bottles, glasses, dry-ice container, mixes— all set in recessed wood mounted on springs.

"What will you gentlemen have?" Elwin asked.

Pete shook his head. "Nothing, thanks."

Ben stepped up and said, "You name it. I'll drink it."

Elwin began bartending with obvious enjoyment. "How about your son, Mr. Moore?"

"He's not twenty-one yet," cautioned Gladys. "Besides he's digging so beautifully."

Pete wondered when he could get Elwin off for a man-to-man talk. He began, "Mr. Luscomb, did you notice your new adobe bricks?"

Elwin shrugged. "That's Gladys's project. Restoration is her baby."

Gladys beamed. "I've been telling them about our house. Come, Mr. Moore, you're an old timer. Tell me if these are good bricks."

Pete followed behind as she hurried across the yard to the back of the house. "I'm getting caught," he mumbled. "I've pooped off most of the day following this redhead around—afoot at that. One more sashay across this damnable yard and I'm doing it horseback."

Gladys was saying, "...so I just set them free with the mud and straw and told them to go to work."

Over his shoulder Pete saw Ben take a few steps after Gladys, wheel and go back to the car with his empty glass.

Three Mexican boys kept mixing reddish-brown clay with straw. Twenty filled molds sat drying in the sun. Stacked on end, off to one side, were several rows of the 3" x 8" x 18" blocks covered with pieces of rusty iron held down by big rocks.

Pete, beginning to question Luscombs' house plans, asked cautiously, "Didn't you say you were going to leave the walls?"

"Those? Oh, yes we are. A complete restoration." She tossed her red hair. "Plus the addition of carport,

29

master bedroom, den, baths, and rumpus room." Her last two words sounded loud in the sudden still of the hot, sultry afternoon, when the tractor motor stopped suddenly.

Fred slid off the seat, vaulted to the ground and called, "I believe I've cleared enough on this end to start hand-digging. It is a single grave, though. Thought I'd find it sooner."

Stumbling over wire and cans, both Luscombs ran to see.

Pete followed slowly.

Ben didn't move from the green sedan's portable bar, where he proceeded to pour himself a drink.

Gladys was at the open grave first. Without a moment's hesitation, she stepped into the shallow pit—her husband right behind.

Pete spoke. "Mr. Luscomb, will you come over to the car a minute where we can talk?"

"Back end is open. Help yourself."

Pete's shoulders sagged.

Fred wiped sweat from his face.

Pete spat in disgust. "C'mon, son, let's go home. The crazy fools are digging faster than flooded gophers. There's no use trying to reason with dudes."

What's A Half-Bull?

Pete Moore, riding horseback near the foot of Saddle Mountain, noticed a curl of white smoke twist upward into the warm summer air. Lifting his weathered chin and flaring the nostrils of his bulbous nose, he sniffed with suspicion. "Burning hair," he mumbled. "Who is branding?" His thoughts raced. *Nobody does range branding so close to home. It's easier to drive to corrals.*

Sensing trouble, Pete reined his horse into the soft sand of a dry wash and rode toward the smoke spiral. A few minutes later the old cowboy rode through a break in mesquite brush and saw the picture.

Buzzard Ben was bent over a large red-and-white calf putting finishing strokes of a brand on the animal's hip.

The calf, mouth open, ran out her tongue and bellowed when the running iron bit past hair and seared skin.

Ben looked up, saw who it was and grinned.

"What in hell do you think you're doing branding one of Luscombs' big calves?" Pete demanded. "You know that animal as well as I do. She's a dead-ringer for her motley-faced mother."

Ben laughed uproariously. "We both know this calf, but I'll bet you five dollars against a pile of cow chips that Elwin will never know." The deft motions of his gnarled hands undid half-hitches of the tie rope. "How can he prove it anyway? There ain't a cow that'll claim this yearlin' past."

As the animal stumbled to her feet, Ben gloated, "This maverick is damn sure wearin' my brand from now on."

Watching the calf dodge and duck into the underbrush, Pete sighed.

Ben kicked dirt onto the small fire. "You heard the redhead accuse us of lettin' the romantic Old West die, didn't you? Well, I'm bringin' a little old-fashioned cattle rustlin' to life."

"You can't get away with too much of it, Ben."

"Not this year anyway," admitted the cowboy. "Old man Johnson has been dead for years, but that nephew of his kept everything branded up pretty good till he sold out."

"Luscomb hired two cowboys out of Tucson," reminded Pete.

Ben coiled his rope and tied it to his saddle. "Shee-ut. I seen them drugstore cowboys. They don't know much more than the Easterner does."

Pete shook his head.

Now see here, you withered ol' son of a bitch," yelled Ben, waving his four-inch-square branding iron in the air to cool it. "Kind of high an' mighty ain't you? You act like you never put your brand on a maverick."

"When I knew who it belonged to?"

"You're the one that wanted Luscomb to leave."

"I still do. It looks to me like you want him to stay

so you can steal everything he owns."

"Quit tryin' to pick a fight. Elwin's got more money than he knows what to do with anyway, an' hell, it ain't even his." Buzzard Ben's eyes were squinted as he looked up. "It's Gladys's money. And what's more, she had it willed to her."

Pete's chin dropped. Where did you get all this crap?"

Ben mounted. "If you hadn't been in such a damn hurry to leave over there last week, you'd of found out plenty yourself. It was funny to watch them dudes hunt for pottery and bones. After dark they stopped diggin'. Hell, they forgot to eat. I was drinkin' and felt so damn good by then I finally told 'em there wasn't no use to expect much pottery, except what the Apaches stole from the Navvys. Dudes is Injun crazy. They get all fired up about anything that has to do with red men. I think they was kind of sad when I told 'em that hole in the yard was a single grave. I told 'em Apaches didn't mess with no graveyard...was always on the move, and if somebody up an' died they chucked him in the ground with all his stuff an' covered him quicker'n a cat...hey! Where are you goin'?"

Pete had reined swiftly and started to ride west.

Ben shouted, "So you ain't interested in Injuns. Well, there's somethin' I ought to let you find out by yourself."

Pete was almost out of earshot, so Ben shortened his story and called, "About half of them one hundred steers the dude turned loose is *bulls*."

If there was a thing Pete Moore was proud of it was his stock. *I buy good bulls and put more'n my share on the open range. When I keep replacement heifers every year, I build up my cows. They're hardy, thrifty, and produce calves that weigh five hundred-fifty pounds off the range every year at shipping time. Dammit, a bunch of poor quality bulls on the range—*

bulls that should be steers—hell, next year's calves'd be lightweight and off-colored. All this went through Pete's mind in one awful flash.

He reined around and called, "How do you know half the steers are bulls?"

"Now you're interested in what the Luscombs is doin', eh?"

"Have you seen them, or are you wild-ass guessing?"

"Both," called Ben. "I seen twenty head the last couple of days, an' half of what I seen was still bulls. So by usin' my third-grade arithmetic an' figurin' if half of what I seen was bulls, than half the whole hundred head must be bulls."

Stunned, Pete rode toward his neighbor.

This time Ben whirled and rode away, taunting, "Stay home a week, cowboy, an' do some ridin' yourself. You'll find most of Luscombs' steers ain't only bulls, they drifted west onto your place." With a parting chuckle, Buzzard Ben rode up the trail toward his headquarters.

Pete's anger flared like a fanned branding fire. Riding downstream he vowed to see for himself. He fumed, "It's hell to sit and let Ben treat me like a dumb hand. That damned old shitass knows I was in Tucson last week, and he knows I haven't really done any riding for two weeks." Pete touched spurs to horse's flanks. "Well, goddammit, I'm riding now."

Pete rode the range all morning. About noon he came onto fifteen head of the dude's steers grazing in a small valley at the foot of Black Mountain. Working alone he couldn't handle them. They were wild and unacclimated in strange country. No one man could drive them.

Inching closer to the bunch, Pete rode to a small knoll within thirty feet of the grazing animals. He leaned forward and looked them over as carefully as a lion watching a herd of deer.

Suddenly he sat straight in the saddle. "That," he said, watching a brindle-colored animal, "is a bull without a doubt." His darting eyes picked out another, and another. Untying his rope, he said to his horse, "We can't get all the one-nut bastards, Dunny, but the ones we do catch will damn sure be steers." He patted the knife in his pocket.

That afternoon Pete rode straight to the Old Johnson Place to confront the Luscombs. He was as mad as a fighting bull himself. Like an enraged bull, he saw nothing but his objective, Elwin. He caught him halfway between the house and the Indian grave hole. "Mr. Luscomb," he said, riding close, "there's a little matter that's got to be threshed out." He held his temper.

"I've been hearing ramifications of that remark for several days, Mr. Moore," was Elwin's haughty answer. "Let's go into the house, sit down as comfortably as possible and discuss the difficulty."

With reluctance, Pete dismounted. He felt safer on his horse. Not waiting to get relaxed and comfortable, he began, "Half...or some," not sure about the number, he hesitated. "A bunch of those steers you turned out on the range are not steers but bulls."

"So Buzzard Ben explained to me," said Elwin, as unimpressed as though his neighbor had announced it was hot weather.

His attitude knocked wind out of Pete almost as hard as a horse kick in the stomach.

The two men walked across the yard. Realizing he was nearing the house where Gladys's presence would force him to watch his language, Pete said, "Goddammit, Mr. Luscomb, do you know what this means?"

"Well, er...ah..." stammered Elwin, misunderstanding

the question, "apparently these poorer quality steers have somehow, in spite of the operation...ah, shall we say retained their potency?"

Pete answered, "I could put it one whole hell of a lot plainer than that, but you get the point."

Mr. Luscomb opened the front door, and the two men went inside. In the process of being remodeled, the house was completely torn up.

Uncomfortable, wondering where Gladys was, Pete straddled a sawhorse.

"As I explained to Buzzard Ben," said Elwin, "I bought the steers in good faith. Assuming they were steers, I had them branded and turned out."

"It always pays a man to look."

"Nevertheless, evidence shows a certain unknown percent of...ah...shall we say these animals are half-bull?"

"Lord no! We can't say that," protested Pete. "There's no such thing as a half-bull. By God, he's a steer all the way, or he's a bull, a whole bull and nothing but a bull."

Elwin teetered on a crate marked GLASS FRAGILE and laughed unexpectedly. "That's what I like about you Westerners. You are independent, uninhibited, and always in character. I propose we drink a toast to the whole bull, the nothing but a bull, so help me—"

"Oh, Ellllwin," Gladys shrieked, entering the room. Her smile was like a snuffed candle when she saw her husband. "My bone china. You are teetering on my—"

Startled, Elwin leaped to his feet, letting the end of the crate hit the wooden floor. He took two steps and sprawled.

Pete grabbed a hammer and loosened the lid of the crate.

Gladys pawed. Wrapping paper and excelsior flew in all directions.

Watching Gladys check her precious collection, Pete wondered why the hubbub. The stuff didn't amount to much in his eyes. It was plainer than white, black-rimmed enamelware and not as practical.

Five minutes later Gladys took a deep sigh and said, "All safe."

"What are you going to do with it now?" asked Pete, his eyes darting around the torn-up house and back to Elwin, who was still on the floor protecting the china as though he were a mother hen with a new batch of chicks.

"Get up, dear," said Gladys. "Nothing is broken."

Elwin slid away from the fragile cups and saucers. He made no attempt to get off his hands and knees until he was three feet away.

"If you men will go outside, I'll repack every piece."

Elwin backed out the front door and sat on the porch.

Pete followed mumbling, "Every time I try to talk sense to these people, something happens and they get me off the subject. They won't get away with it this time. I'm not going home. Not yet." He looked Elwin in the eye. Then he spoke tersely through his clenched store-bought teeth, "This bull business is a serious matter."

Elwin squirmed on the rickety step.

"Do you know what our calves will look like if those bulls of yours are left on the range?" Pete demanded. When Elwin didn't attempt a description, Pete raised his voice. "They'll look worse than a cross between a javelina hog and an old brush fence."

Elwin's eyes rolled upward. "I can't visualize—"

"I have good quality Hereford bulls," Pete interrupted. "So does Buzzard Ben." He squatted on his boot heels and leaned his back against a post. "You, Mr. Luscomb, have one."

"One bull on this whole ranch?" Elwin seemed to take the fact as an insult.

Pete shrugged. "Don't worry. There's plenty of bulls to go around. It's open range country between us." Pride sounded in his voice. "And I run good bulls."

Elwin leaped to his feet. "This situation is intolerable. I shall stop everything and take care of the matter personally."

Standing to face the taller man, Pete shouted, "God, no!"

"Yes," Elwin shouted louder. "I mean to drive to Tucson tomorrow and purchase the best Hereford bulls money can buy."

"We don't especially need more bulls," insisted Pete. "It's getting rid of the sorry bastards—" He stopped his flow of words abruptly and glanced around to see if Gladys were within earshot. *Dammit, why can't a dude get on a horse and ride out in the open air where a man can let his talk be as free and easy as water rolling down a sand wash.*

Elwin cleared his throat loudly and pulled at the back of his plaid cowboy shirt as though searching for a courtroom coattail. "Reviewing the aspects of the case, I have steers, that is, bulls on the range that must be castrated at the earliest opportunity. A simple operation of necessity must be performed. We merely, then, need to drive said animals to headquarters."

"Yeah, and who's going to drive them?"

"I have hired two cowboys."

"Oh, no, don't turn them loose. They don't know this rough, bushy country. They'll run the wild cattle into the mesquite thickets. We'll be three years smoking them out."

"Perhaps, Mr. Moore, you can suggest an alternative?"

Pete seized the opportunity. "Sell out. I'll buy them.

I'll gather them."

Elwin spat out the words, "No. Never." Chameleon-like he changed to outer smoothness. "Could I persuade you to help in gathering my steers?"

The hopelessness of his position reached Pete at last. His stomach churned. He tasted bile. His thoughts raced. *If I don't help, my range plan for better calves is ruined. If I do help, I'll be working for a greenhorn. I'd rather be caught between a kicking horse and a barn door.*

After a pause, Elwin said, "I will naturally make it worth your while."

Pete winced. "I work for myself."

"Of course." Elwin wiped perspiration from his forehead. "No offense meant. This insufferable heat! My wife doesn't mind it, but I will be relieved when our air conditioner is installed." He motioned toward the kitchen. "Are you positive you wouldn't care for an afternoon cocktail?"

Curling and re-curling his hat brim, Pete shook his head. Shoulders drooped, he stepped off the porch and settled his Stetson low on his bald head. Over his shoulder he said, "I'll help you gather the steers."

Walking toward his horse, he looked into the sky and beseeched, "God, is it true? Me, Pete Moore, wrangling half-bulls for a son-of-a-bitchin' dude?"

The Dude's
Pasture Sissies

It was almost sundown the middle of July. Pete and Ben were driving a bunch of Hereford cattle home to Pete's range. As they neared the river crossing at the Old Johnson Place, Ben pulled alongside Pete's horse. "I almost forgot to tell you," he said, "Elwin wants to show you his surprise."

"Deal me out. Another hundred feet along the edge of this thicket and I'm on clear ground to home."

Ben stopped. "Talk about the devil...." He pointed to a pool of water below the crossing. "Get a load of that."

Elwin and Gladys Luscomb were attempting to pull a cow out the mud. Both had their lariats around her horns and were straining their horses against the ropes.

Ben guffawed. "Those damn fools couldn't pull a drowned rat out of a water trough."

"I have to get these cattle home," Pete said. "Go over there and show them how to get a cow out of the bog."

"The hell! The way Elwin's goin', he'll wind up in the bog hisself."

"My God!" yelled Pete, looking closer at the scene. "That's one of my cows. Hold these cattle for me here, and I'll get their ropes off her."

Gladys and Elwin looked up at the same time.

"What are you trying to do?" Pete called, "Kill her?" Sliding off his horse, he inched his boots along the shaking, watery sand. The struggling cow had worked water from the river silt under her hoofs and had become hopelessly mired.

Unfastening the Luscombs' ropes and tossing them free, Pete tied his own catch rope around the cow's neck. With his bare hands he dug away the packed silt from around each hoof.

Elwin dismounted and helped Pete dig.

At last Pete mounted and turned his horse away from the cow.

Easing his mount forward in a steady pull, he took the slack out of the rope and pulled the cow free. He dropped the rope and turned.

"Amazing," called Elwin. He sounded more like a circus ringmaster than a lawyer. Running downstream, he tried to catch the cow by the trailing rope.

"Get horseback," Pete yelled.

His warning came too late. The cow, head low, turned and charged the Easterner. Elwin clawed his way up the riverbank, as the cow bawled and hooked her horns at him from behind.

Pete loped his horse between them and nodded in relief when the rope slid off her curved horns and flipped into the mesquite thicket.

41

Ben, laughing his loudest, sat watching the show.

Pete scooped up his rope, reined his horse across the river and regrouped his cattle. "Damn it. I spent a week gathering and corralling these sonsabitches. I sure want to get them home."

Circling automatically and helping hold the cattle in a bunch, Ben was still laughing. "Every time that dude makes a move he gets hisself into a cryin' scrape. He always steppin' on his...." Last words were lost as he slapped his chaps. "Look at him run. Hell, he's goin' to beat his wife and horse home."

Pete, leaving the scene with his cattle, crossed the riverbed and turned south.

"Don't forget to meet me at Luscombs' the evenin' of the seventh for the big surprise," was Ben's parting call.

Pete snorted. "A dude can't do anything to surprise me anymore." He glanced at his gnarled hands, so clean from being washed in wet sand. *Why can't I get the Easterners off my hands?*

Two nights later Pete reluctantly saddled up and rode east. If he didn't check up on the so-called surprise for himself, he'd either worry about what the Easterner was up to or he'd have to get it secondhand from Ben.

On the way to the Old Johnson Place he noticed one of Ben's favorite bulls, a large, hardy Hereford, horned and of good range quality. "As long as I'm headed that way," he said, talking to the animal as though he were a dear old friend, "I'll drive you back toward your own range. Go on, hi ya, hit the trail, you split-eared old buck-ox."

Riding past the adobe, Pete rode to the corrals where Gladys, Elwin and Buzzard Ben were sitting on the ground, backs against the railroad-tie fence.

Pegged out in front of them was a long, heavy, pine board over one foot wide and two inches thick. Coiled on the board was about thirty feet of Manila rope.

"Howdy," said Gladys and Elwin together with studied nonchalance.

Buzzard Ben, watching Gladys, raised his hand, said nothing.

Swinging off his horse, Pete thought, *What does that old bastard do, live over here?* He acknowledged the Luscombs' greetings and added, "Ben said you had something to show me."

Elwin grabbed up a dishpan of rolled oats.

"Just a minute, dear," Gladys pleaded. "The surprise will keep for a few more minutes. Maybe Mr. Moore has a suggestion for us about naming our ranch."

Pete sighed and squatted on his heels.

Gladys spread her palms upward. "For days I've tried to find a name for this ranch—one that would be fitting, unique, romantic, and personal."

Pete scratched the side of his big nose. "You don't need a new name. Everybody knows this is the Old Johnson Place." He put equal stress on all words.

"It's our place now," reminded Gladys. "I'm afraid the old name won't do."

Ben wriggled his back to another position against the corral fence. "I been settin' here half an hour givin' 'em ideas, but they don't like none of em."

Flipping the loose rope end, Gladys made a capital *'L'* and placed it flat on the smooth pine board.

Pete eyed the $7/16$ ths Manila rope with satisfaction. "Good quality, right size. It'll make a dandy catch rope."

Ben chuckled. "This rope won't never catch nothin'. It's for makin' letters on her sign."

"Our housewarming is next month," Gladys explained. "We must have a name."

"Don't look at me," said Pete, tugging his hat brim lower on his forehead. "Ours is the Moore Ranch; to the west is Buzzard Ben's Outfit, and this is the Old Johnson Place." He hoped the words sounded as definite and final as he meant them. He raised his head and looked Elwin Luscomb straight in the eye. "Ben said you had something important on your mind."

"I certainly have. Gladys, where did you put the pan of rolled oats?"

"You are holding it."

"So I am. Now," he said, rising as though ready to face a jury, "watch this. I don't want you to miss even the beginning of my surprise."

Carrying the large pan, he left the horse corral and strode to the wire gate of the barbed wire pasture, a ten-acre, brush-fringed piece of land between the corrals and the river.

The others stood and followed. Gladys turned and smiled knowingly at Pete who looked at his scuffed boots and straightened a spur.

Ben put his shoulder to the handle and unlatched the wire gate, a panel in the fence braced by two staves. It sagged and fell to the ground as soon as its tension was gone. Elwin stepped forward, Ben next and then Gladys. Pete pulled up the slack-wire panel from the ground, closed the gap in the fence and twisted bailing wire around the post and latch to hold the gate shut.

Inside the pasture Elwin said, "You three stand quietly and observe." Moving a few paces away, he began shaking the pan of rolled oats and calling, "Here bullzies, come on bullzies." His voice was loud and coaxing.

"Watch," instructed Gladys. "They'll come. They have every evening since we bought them."

A few calls later, three large, red-and-white bulls ambled out of the brush single file toward Elwin. The Easterner shook the pan invitingly. "That's right. Good bullzies. Nice bullzies." He put the pan on the ground and struck a dramatic pose, chin raised, arms opened wide, as though he had produced not one, but three star witnesses. "Did you ever," he said with exultation, "set eyes on three Hereford bulls with more class than these?"

Pete studied the square-built animals. "Not outside a show ring."

"But we don't run cattle like that on the range," said Ben.

Gladys beamed. "We will now. These are the most beautiful creatures I have ever seen. We are proud to make this addition to the range."

Elwin let his chest swell. "Which bull would you men say is best?"

"Best for what?" asked Ben, hitching up his pants.

"Point for point," said Elwin. "Surely you cowmen know how to judge a prize bull?"

"We judge a bull by how many calves he gets, how he covers the country, and how much he enjoys his work." Remembering Gladys, Pete stopped explaining and thought, *It sure looks like ladies would leave when men are talking private.*

Elwin pointed to the animals in turn and with patronizing tone said, "We shall name them Bull Number One, Bull Number Two, and Bull Number Three. Which would you say is most expensive?"

"If you intended to buy range bulls," mumbled Pete to himself, "whatever you gave was too much."

"What did you say, Pete?" Elwin insisted. "Pick one."

Buzzard Ben interrupted. "I can tell a good bull from a poor bull, but these classy, hand-fed pasture...well, all's I can say is..." pointing to Bull Number Three, "that bull there has got the most sense."

"I fooled you," gloated Elwin. "He's the least expensive. I paid only two thousand for him."

The cowboys cleared their throats. Pete's blue eyes slid away from Ben's brown eyes. Both men shrugged.

"Bull Number Two cost five thousand." Elwin rocked back on his heels. "Bull Number Three, four thousand."

Gladys stroked prize Bull Number Two's white face and scratched him behind the left ear.

"He hasn't got a head on him as good as the one Ben picked," said Pete.

"My dear man," explained Elwin, "one does not select bulls by the shape of the head." He ran the flat of his hand along the bull's back and down the square-shaped rump. "The meat is here. It is where we check an animal's potential beef-making qualities."

"I have bulls," Pete said evenly, "and one with a good head means easier handling and sensible calves."

"Yeah," added Ben. "Buy a bull that's wide between the eyes, an' let him have lots of get up an' go like my split-eared bull. He—"

"Easy Ben," warned Pete, cocking his head toward Gladys. Turning again to Elwin he agreed, "I'm sure they're worth the money, but I can't figure, considering what you need here on this ranch...well, what are they for?"

Elwin stuck his right trouser leg inside his black alligator boot. After a moment he slapped his thigh and laughed. "What are these bulls for? I understand now. You men are joking, of course. That's pretty good. Sometimes I am slow catching on to your Western-type humor." He forced another laugh.

Ben ran a thumb down his long nose. "We ain't jokin', Mr. Luscomb," he said slowly. "Are you keepin' 'em for pets?"

Elwin put an arm around the neck of Bull Number Two and helped Gladys scratch his ears. "They are part of my range plan."

There was studied patience in his voice. "Mr. Moore, you informed me I had only one bull. I am sure there were six listed when I bought the place. I found later I was taking advantage of my neighbors by not having bulls for my own ranch."

"But you haven't bought *range* bulls," said Pete, matching patience for patience.

"No," agreed Ben. "You sure can't turn these loose on this rough country."

"Why not?" asked Elwin.

"Because they're used to being fed," said Pete. They'd starve on the range."

"He-men like these?"

Buzzard Ben smothered a chuckle. "An' not only that, my ol' split-eared bull would muck out on these pasture sissies before they could bellar an' run."

Elwin clenched his fingers in the curly coat of the prize bull. "I don't believe you men know good bulls when you see them." He whirled, his anger showing. "They possess all the attributes of fine bulls—short legs, flat backs, wide tails, heavy hams—class, class, *class*!"

"Yeah," said Ben, "but like we said, can they rustle food 'n stuff?"

"You men are attempting to belittle my purchase," roared Elwin.

"Not at all," soothed Pete. "Now they're real pretty. And you could use them in a cooler climate on good grass. They'll even be all right here as long as you keep them in the pasture and feed them."

"'Course the cows is out in rough hills," reminded Ben.

"Then the cows can come here," said Elwin.

"Maybe your cows is different than mine," said Ben. "My cows—" Feeling Pete's jab in the ribs, he stopped talking.

Bull Number One and Bull Number Three kept nosing the feed pan over and over. Gladys, not talkative as usual, helped Elwin stroke his five-thousand-dollar prize.

From outside the fence came the loud trumpeting of another bull.

Ben said, "Well stick me full of needles an' call me a porkypine, if it ain't ol' Split-ear. Hi, there, boy, where you been?"

"I think he came down off Black Mountain," Pete answered. "I pushed him up the trail as I rode over here today." It took him one glance at the Luscombs to decide they were not pleased to see old Split-ear.

Gladys stood behind Elwin, and Elwin stood behind his best bull.

Ben started for the fence. "Let's open up the gate an' show what we mean by a range bull. An' ol' Split-ear ain't ornery neither. We ain't had no fighters on the range for the last twenty-five years. Hit the fence everybody! C'mon, Pete, fork your horse."

"Stop!" cried Elwin. "Take your bull and get off my property."

Gladys put a restraining hand on Elwin's arm. "Please, dear."

Ben took hold of the wire gate. "Wait up. If by *property* you mean this patented land"—he drew a circle with his forefinger around the buildings, corrals, and land along the river—"sure, we'll move on out, but my bull goes anywhere he wants to on this leased rangeland."

Old Split-ear pawed the ground.

"Take that bull home!" thundered Elwin, fixing Ben with what must have been his best courtroom stare.

Ben looked down his long nose. "On an open range, you have to fence my bull off your place, if you don't want him around."

Ben's words were almost drowned out as the three new bulls pawed the ground and began trumpeting on their own. Noise grew louder when fighting cries rose to full blast.

Pete climbed through the barbed-wire fence and jumped into his saddle—left toe in stirrup, right leg swung over.

Elwin, backing up, stepped into the empty feed pan, lost his balance and fell on his backside.

When Gladys began screaming, Ben threw his arms around her. He managed a half squeeze before she ducked and ran for the four-strand, barbed-wire fence. Not slacking her pace, she made a dive between the second and third strands, snagged her shirt front and kept going.

Elwin picked himself off the ground and followed her.

All four bulls trumpeted together. The dust grew thicker. Pete felt grains between his teeth, and his eyes smarted. "It's a shame to have to break this up." Reining his horse close to the bull, he called, "Go on, you split-eared old devil. Get on back to the top of the mountain. These pasture sissies aren't going to cut in on your territory. Hi ya, go on."

Old Split-ear didn't pay any attention. He continued to stand, bellow, and paw dirt over his back.

Pete untied a small rope from his saddle and flipped the bull in the face to distract him. "Ben," he called, "come on."

Ben was already over the fence and on his horse. Together he and Pete turned the bull and drove him off into the mesquite thicket.

Although Ben reined toward the corrals, Pete rode another hundred feet before he convinced himself he should return and see if all was well with the Luscombs.

Gladys, shying away from Ben's offer of assistance, kept repeating, "Help Elwin." She made futile attempts to hold her shredded blouse together.

Ben said, "Pete, *you* help Elwin."

Pete dismounted and went to the rescue.

Elwin was caught in the barbed-wire fence. One of his feet was on the east side of the bottom wire, and the other, the west. His head hung between wires three and four, the back of his hair twisted in a sharp barb.

When Pete pulled out his large pocket knife and flipped open the longest blade, Elwin yelped. Without bothering to explain, Pete stepped up the fence and whacked off the tangled lock of hair. Snapping the blade closed, he dropped the knife back into his pocket and reached for the fence. By spreading the wires farther apart, he gave Elwin room to step free. When he did, Gladys rushed forward.

Ben remarked, "You sure must have been duckin' low an' fast."

The three fancy bulls retreated into the mesquite-fringed pasture, and except for an occasional bawl, they grew quiet.

Elwin said, "I'm going to the house for a drink. This incident has frayed my nerves."

"It's frayed the back of your britches, too," said Ben.

Gladys, still clutching torn sections of her shirt front in an attempt to cover a heaving bosom, said in a quavering voice, "Let's all go to the house."

Pete and Ben said, "No, thanks," in unison. Ben added, "Time's awastin'. We gotta hit the trail."

The two men rode off side by side. Out of earshot, Pete said, "So that's a dude surprise. If Elwin's here a year from now, I'll have to remember to ask him about his pet bulls. That is, *if* he's still here."

Flying GL/Her Brand

Toward the end of July weather on the San Pedro River grew muggier. It was rainy season, but so far only scattered showers had fallen on the rangelands. Electrical storms at the head of the San Pedro sent flash floods roaring past the ranches, leaving soggy mud banks and pools of muddy water in the wide river bed after the high water flowed on north.

Riding upstream before sunup Pete and son Fred drove ten head of the dude's big steers back toward the Luscomb range. About a hundred yards from the river crossing they pulled up sharply. Gladys Luscomb galloped toward them on her black horse.

Pete said, "What is it about dudes that makes them go everywhere at a high lope?"

Fred shrugged. "Probably think that's the way to work. Watch. She rides well, but I wonder who told her to have her stirrups so high. She looks like an overweight jockey trying to catch the pack."

"Circle these steers," warned Pete. "We'll have to keep them bunched if we want to get them all to the other side."

"Too late, Dad. Come on. Let's push them on across."

"Right at her?"

"She'll turn."

But Gladys didn't. Riding at full gallop, she reined her black horse into the center of the steers.

"God Almighty, Fred, is that redhead blind?"

"It's all right. The steers aren't going to run her down. At least they are spreading out and giving her the middle of the crossing."

The steers began climbing the west bank, and Gladys galloped on across, heading east.

"She's not that stubborn," said Pete. "The way she's riding, her husband must have wrecked his car and killed himself."

The two men pulled their horses to a stop and called together, "What's the trouble?"

"Oh," she gasped, stopping and reaching into the breast pocket of her cowboy shirt, "I'm so upset. Elwin brought the mail from town last night. I wanted to come right over to your place, but it was too late, so I started this morning with this." She waved a letter, motioning for Pete to take it.

He leaned out of his saddle and took the envelope. His first thoughts were, *Maybe the deed is not clear. Maybe her money is no good. Maybe the Easterners haven't bought the Old Johnson Place after all.*

"Open it," Gladys urged. "Read and tell me what I can do."

Obligingly, Pete shook the paper from the envelope and, holding a single white sheet at arm's length, read to himself. Handing the paper to Fred, he said to Gladys, "You mean you rode right into the middle of a bunch of 'boogery' steers to bring me that?"

"Why...why yes. As you can see, it's from the Livestock Sanitary Board. I've been waiting for three weeks for them to record my brand. This letter says the brand belongs to somebody else." Her lips trembled. Her voice cracked. "I can't use it." She took back her letter. "What can I do?"

"That's easy, Mrs. Luscomb," said young Fred. "Be practical. Figure out another brand."

"There is no other brand but G L for me. My initials."

Pete and Fred looked at each other, eyebrows raised.

"Not only that, I've already had my branding irons made. I've waited years to put G L on a calf, and I won't give up."

She tossed her red hair and stamped her foot in the right stirrup. The black horse reared and whirled. She caught the reins, regained her balance and galloped back across the river toward her headquarters.

Pete shook his head. "I don't expect common sense from a dude, but that beats the pee-wadding out of anything I ever saw. Initials! No cattle brand is any good except her initials. She doesn't want a brand, she wants a monogram."

"Come on," called Fred. "She's waving for us to follow."

"The hell. I'll be damned if I'll follow. I don't feel very neighborly today."

"O.K., Dad. Shall we ride up to Indian Springs and see if that last little shower in the mountains put any water in the new dirt tank?"

"No, go on home, then take some salt to the cattle out on Black Mountain." Pete slowed his mount. "So long." As he jogged along the narrowing trail, he called, "I'll move off here in the brush and see if I run onto any cattle with worms, and I hope to hell I don't see any of Elwin's big steers that aren't steers."

"Yeah," Fred shouted, "keep an eye out for any half-bulls."

"Not funny," Pete shouted back. "We probably didn't get all those one-nut bastards." He rode through the mesquite thicket and returned to the river crossing.

Content the Luscombs were nowhere in sight, he forded the river and rode along the bank until he came to a spring that supplied the only water for irrigating the sixty acres of the Old Johnson Place. Pete chuckled to himself with satisfaction, knowing it was his spring and leased by him to the Luscombs one year at a time.

A man knelt at the spring drinking water from his cupped hands. Morning sunlight hit the top of his scraggly hair. Pete hailed him, asking, "Hunting more mavericks?"

"Watch it," Ben said. "Don't nobody find much un-branded stuff when you're ridin'." He sat up and pulled his wide hat brim down over his eyes. "No. I was just killin' time. Elwin is goin' to Tucson today, an' I'm waitin' around till he leaves before I go over an' help Gladys."

Pete dismounted. "I'll bet that redhead needs your help about as much as I need another no-good son-in-law."

"That's all you know about it. I helped her figure out a brand. I named the ranch for her—at least I tried to. An' I dug her up a dead Injun." He leaned back on one elbow and chuckled. "I tell you, Pete, I get a kick out of them Luscombs. They're funnier than two skunks at a picnic. An' dumb?"

"They're not dumb, and they're not funny to me. It hurts to watch Elwin get in one crying scrape after another."

"Not the redhead though. I was at the ranch last

week helpin' her figure out a brand so she could use her initials. I follered her into the barn, when she went to get her brandin' irons to show me. I made a grab for those great tits, an' thought I had her, but she's fast. She ducked behind a stack of red salt blocks. There she was, an' there I was. 'Gladys,' I says, to ease her mind an' to get her to stop dodgin' like a cow in a mesquite thicket, 'I see you bought iodized salt for the cattle to lick.' She was puffin' some, but she pushed a block over to the other side of that little barn an' sat on it. 'I did?' she says. She laughed that gurgling laugh of hers. Said she didn't know nothin' about iodized. She said she just looked at the white blocks, the yellow blocks, an' the bee-utiful red-rust ones. 'Course she bought the red ones because they matched the landscape. Now, ain't that a dinger? Everythin' with a damn dude is for show and blow."

Pete squatted on the ground and began rolling a cigarette. "How did Gladys get out of the barn?"

"While I was tellin' her about the sulphur in the yellow blocks, she just picked up the two brandin' irons, held 'em in front of her an' backed out the door. Then she sat on a big rock an' held the irons out in front of her. I was bidin' my time, so I squatted down on my hunkers and leaned back comfortable against the side of the barn. She dug the G and the L into the ground and said like this" Ben continued falsetto, "'I guess I should have checked before I had these irons made up, but I didn't, and I'd still like to use my initials.'"

Pete almost choked on a lung full of smoke. "You sound just like that Eastern woman."

"Hell, I asked her why she didn't turn her G around

backwards. She was real tickled about that till I told her the brand would be called Crazy G L. She wrinkled her forehead nice and pretty before she said, 'I don't like the sound of *crazy*.' Dropping his voice into its normal gruffness, Ben added, "So I told her to put the G on its back and call her brand the Lazy G L. She looked unhappy till I told her she sure wasn't lazy, an' I didn't think the name fit. I said to try mixin' up the letters like Crazy G, Lazy L; or Lazy G, Crazy L. I could tell I wasn't gettin' nowheres, so I just said to make the damn brand Crazy all the way whether it fit or not."

"Did she agree?"

"Naw." Her temper was beginnin' to blaze to match her hair. I rolled on my back and waved my boots in the air. Sure enough, I told her I was teasin'. If she wanted to add bars an' slashes an' stuff, there was millions of combinations. I guess she knowed she needed help, 'cause she simmered down some. She even smiled real pretty. She kept sayin' she only wanted to use her 'nitials for her brand. When I told her there was rockin' letters, flyin' letters...that done it! Right there she reared up so happy I thought she was gonna kiss me." Ben paused and looked down his long nose, sighed and admitted, "But she didn't. She slid off the rock, dropped them irons, and picked up a couple of twigs from the ground. 'Wings,' she squeals. Then she asks me how to make her brand fly. At least that gave me a chance to edge up close. I made a grab for her hand. She stuck those two little sticks into my fist and told me to put wings on both letters."

"Dudes never know when to quit. Wings on the G is enough."

"That's what I told her and Elwin...yeah, Elwin.

Wouldn't you know the damned husband would show up. Well, I didn't get nothin'—not so much as a squeeze, but Gladys wound up with a pretty good open brand, by droppin' the L down below the G an' connectin' it." Ben drew the Flying G L on the soft ground.

Pete leaned forward and flexed his knees. "Aren't the Luscombs keeping the brand they bought with the place?"

"Sure. This new Flyin' G L is to be Gladys's own personal brand for her calves."

"What calves?"

"The dairy calves she's goin' to raise next spring. She's ordered some cows." Ben resettled his hat. "Holsteins."

"I'll bet old man Johnson is turning over in his grave. He wouldn't allow a milk cow on the place."

"That reminds me," said Ben, standing and stretching his legs. "The ranch ain't to be knowed as the Old Johnson Place no more."

"By God," Pete exploded, "that's damn sure what I'll call it."

"Don't make no difference. Gladys has a new name, an' the signs'll be up in a day or two."

"More than one?"

Ben walked a few feet from the spring to where backwash formed little eddies. Watercress grew in the slow-moving water. Picking several long stems, he sat on the bank of the irrigating ditch and took a bite of the fresh green leaves. "Yep, there'll be a sign on the road where she joins up with you on the west, another one where me an' her joins up on the east, plus a hell of a big sign over the gate as you drive off the main road an' into her yard at headquarters."

After a few minutes of silence, Ben continued,

"Ain'tcha goin' to take the bait? Don'tcha want to know what she calls her ranch? I'll give you a clue. She says she tied the name in with her Indian diggins."

"They can call it Luscombs' Folly or Ye Oldy Holy in the Ground, but I'll always say, the Old Johnson Place."

Several minutes passed without conversation.

"This watercress is sure good," said Ben, reaching for a double handful. "I don't blame Gladys for comin' down here an' pickin' so much. She sure likes the stuff. Says when she has her housewarmin' she's goin' to have a stack of itsy-bitsy watercress sandwiches this high." He raised his right arm and spread his hands a foot apart.

Pete didn't care. He was busy thinking about how the Luscombs were using the water from his spring to wet their sixty acres...how they were picking his watercress...putting up signs...letting extra steers eat his feed. To himself he vowed that next year he would refuse to sign the lease. He would divert the spring water, then maybe the dudes would quit playing cowboy and go back East where they belonged.

Ben squinted at the sun. "Only eight o'clock. Shee-ut." He spat over the irrigation ditch onto the mud of the wide riverbed. "Elwin won't even be up yet. It'll be another hour before he'll get his ass off for Tucson. That's one thing you'll have to give the red credit for. She's the first dude woman I ever seen that'd rise and shine before mid-mornin'."

Pete snorted. "You brag about all the tail you get, but how much do you know about sleeping habits of dude women?"

"A damn sight more'n you do, you withered old prune. All right, you don't need to swaller your damned store teeth. If I want to play a stack of chips at the redhead, I'll damn sure do it. I don't see as how you're doin' so well gettin' rid of 'em like you bragged you would." Ben shrugged. "The way I see it, if you can't fight 'em, screw 'em." He threw back his head and guffawed. "Don't Elwin tickle your funny bone?"

"Not much."

"Wait till you see him again. He's hopped up on Apache Injuns now he's found that burial mound."

"Are they still digging the hole in their front yard?"

"Sure, an' in a new one I found in the mesquite brush along their pasture fence. Elwin's readin' up on Apaches, too."

Pete swung onto his horse. "Some of those wild, bloodthirsty stories about the bad men of the Southwest might give that dude some ideas about how to take care of *you*."

Ben mounted and yanked his hat brim. "He already thinks he's too damn smart. The other day I says to call their place *Tiswin*. Pete, they was all for it. Gladys thinks it sounds real Injun. 'Course I lets on it means Cheers, Hello, or Goodbye. Gladys figures *Tiswin* is the local word for Aloha. Least that's what she says. She an' Elwin goes 'round the whole day sayin' *Tiswin* an' havin' a good time loopin' that new Manila rope on the board to spell it out for their sign."

When Pete didn't respond, Ben continued, "Next day Elwin must of looked it up when he went to Tucson, 'cause the next time I got over there he gives me that cold stare of his and says, '*Tiswin* is Apache whisky. It is powerful. It makes everybody drunk. It causes trouble.'

"I still thought it was a damn good name, original and romantic like Gladys wanted. Naturally, I told 'em I liked the name they picked better. I even held the bucket while they varnished over the rope on the sign board."

Pete didn't ask what Luscombs had named their ranch, and when Ben told him he'd see him at the housewarming, he spurred his horse and called over his shoulder, "You won't see me there eating itsy-bitsy watercress sandwiches and drinking store-bought *Tiswin*. If you catch me around those Easterners again, it'll be because I'm trapped."

Housewarming

Pete Moore stretched in an old leather chair and squinted at late afternoon sun through the porch screen of their adobe ranch house. "Housewarming," he grumbled to his wife and son. "I'll repeat myself. If you see me around those damned dudes again, it'll be because I'm trapped."

"Come on, Dad," urged young Fred. "Nothing is going on around here, and I have to go back to school in six weeks."

"You and your mother go. Those Easterners beat me out of that cow outfit, and I'm feeling about as neighborly as a cornered Gila monster. Only way a housewarming at Luscombs' hacienda would interest me is if everything over there got as hot as Mexican chili and burnt up." He ground his cigarette out in a jar lid and snorted. "So Gladys and Elwin restored the Old Johnson Place, fine, but they ruined it as far as I'm concerned."

Fred put his hand on his father's shoulder. "They ruined it for Buzzard Ben, too. They kept him from buying the place, but he's not holding a grudge."

"He's too busy playing a stack of chips at Elwin's wife. He'd better leave that buxom redhead alone." Pete turned to his slender wife, leaning against the weathered door jamb. "Pearl, why do you want to mix with those people?"

Slanting rays of sunlight touched high cheekbones of her smooth-skinned face. "We are invited to their party. I want to go."

Fred faced his father. "Don't you think we ought to be polite?"

Pearl flipped her long gray-streaked braid and stepped beside Fred. "Our daughters and their families are going, and all dressed up."

Pete reached for his new boots. He started to say, *All right. I'll go, but I have a hunch stronger than reboiled coffee that before the evening is over, I'll wish I'd stayed here and watched for clouds. My feet hurt. It's going to rain.*

Instead, he stared at his wife. "I almost forgot how pretty you are."

A few minutes later the Moores started up the road in a faded blue pickup toward the Old Johnson Place. Fred drove; Pete sat by the window, and Pearl settled between them. She kept easing her full skirt around the gear shift and smoothing the front ruffles of her purple satin blouse as they left headquarters of their ranch, crossed the small stream of San Pedro River and proceeded up the rutty road.

They approached a sign suspended from two short chains fastened to a mesquite post. Spelled out in two lines with rope tacked to a 2' x 12' board were the words:

63

Entering The Wickiup Ranch
Elwin and Gladys Luscomb

After reading aloud, Fred remarked, "We're on foreign ground. Does anyone feel different?"

"I've felt different ever since we passed the year nineteen-hundred and aught-six. And, of course, I feel different when I'm around dudes." He tugged at his wide hat brim and spat out the word: "Wickiup. It wouldn't have surprised me for the Luscombs to call the Old Johnson Place the Crazy or Lazy something or other, but why The Wickiup?"

"Because Elwin is full steam ahead about anything he feels is Apache."

The truck lurched to the right as it swerved to avoid a chuckhole. When the engine coughed, Fred said, "Dad we need to have this truck overhauled before a valve breaks and throws a piston through the crankcase."

Pete grunted. Pearl kept her silence.

For the next two miles there was only the sound of the uneven running of the motor. Nearing the Old Johnson Place, Pete said, "Noisy bunch. Guess the party has been going on a few hours already. At least we'll not be noticed in the crowd."

Fred turned sharply to the left and drove under a huge sign similar to the one they passed on the road. This sign, with the ranch brand burned into the wood free hand with a running iron, was also written in rope. It read:

The Wickiup
Gladys & Elwin

Rounding the turn beyond the gate, Pete gasped. "This can't be the Old Johnson Place. I'm lost."

Fred skidded the truck to a stop. "It is The Wickiup now."

"Well, it doesn't look like any round-topped, brush-covered Apache wickiup I ever saw."

"Wow, potted flowers. Floodlights. Fitted sod. They must have hired a whole crew to do all this work at the last minute."

Pearl wondered aloud. "Where did all the cars and people come from?"

"Must be over two hundred, counting kids," Pete mumbled, wrinkled chin sagging.

Fred shrugged. "You know how it is when you say free food, free drinks, come one, come all. This must be an open house as well as a housewarming."

At that moment, Gladys, who seemed to be floating between the outdoor tables, looked up and saw the truck. Tripping toward the Moores, she called her welcome. "We are so glad you came...our favorite neighbors." She stopped, letting yards and yards of pink net skirt swirl gracefully around her matching high-heeled slippers.

Several local people glanced around and called greetings to the new arrivals.

"Don't know half of them," Pete mumbled to his wife. "Must be Tucson folks."

Gladys gave parking instructions. "So if you'll back your car out beyond the gate, we'll have all this open clearing for square dancing later on."

Obediently Fred spun truck wheels and roared out to the designated area.

Helping Pearl from the car, Pete said, "If I had known the redhead was going to make me walk half way to her housewarming, I'd have rode my horse."

Obviously enjoying her role as hostess, Gladys re-greeted the Moores and led them a zigzag path through the outdoor tables. Grasping Pearl's arm as though she were a childhood chum, she said, "I've met your four lovely daughters. Aren't you fortunate in having them all married and living within fifty miles? My daughter is away at school." Turning to Pete, she added, "And I like your sons-in-law."

Pete found his voice. "I don't claim any of them. The daughters, yes, but those four men are my *wife's* sons-in-law."

"How delightful," murmured Gladys, leading the three. "I'm sure you are acquainted with many of our guests, but I want you to meet some of our Tucson friends." She smiled graciously.

"And I want them to know you."

Fred and Gladys stepped ahead. Pete lagged with Pearl. "Yes," he whispered, "there's nothing I'd rather do than meet some more dudes."

Ten minutes later Gladys led the Moores into the house. "I know you'll be interested in seeing how we carried out our plans, but first, come sample our buffet."

Pete's shaggy eyebrows raised and blue eyes wid-ened. He looked in vain for beans—searched for barbecue. "Not even a goat," he whispered to Pearl. "This isn't a housewarming, it's a ladies' tea. Sand-wiches aren't ranch style. These trays of stuff look

66

interesting but darn sure unfamiliar. At Pearl's insistence, he nibbled at a cracker spread with a foreign substance. "Fishy," he said, swallowing hard.

There were so many people inside the house it was impossible to do much but move sideways. Most of the children were out of doors where there was room to run. Fred and Pearl were soon lost in the crowd. Pete retreated to the west wall where Elwin was giving some sort of lecture to six or seven listening strangers. Pete inched forward until he was close enough to hear.

"It is now thought," came Elwin's voice, "that Apache and Navajo were an undifferentiated people not many centuries ago, but that the latter, on occupying the San Juan drainage between the several branches of the pueblo, absorbed more culture from closer contact with these relatively advanced peoples, and gradually...."

Pete backed out of earshot. Feeling a tap on his shoulder, he turned. "Hello, Ben. You're right. Elwin has been reading up on Indians and probably eating loco weed."

Glassy-eyed, Pete's neighbor said, "I been waitin' a couple of hours to ask you somethin', but I have to show you first."

Pete, following Buzzard Ben, greeted several cowboys and talked with a neighbor named Gonzalez before he was again within earshot of Elwin's lecture.

The Easterner's voice was louder, "...on the basis of anthropometric observations, but display a distinctive physiognomy which is perhaps to be interpreted as the reflection of their habits, of mind and life—not to mention...."

Ben nudged Pete. "That's the third time he's told the same story this afternoon, first to one damn bunch of dudes, then another."

Elwin reached behind a large silver bowl on the mantel and brought out a partially destroyed skull. "Most Indian ruins—that is to say, 'diggings,' produce only fragments of pottery or arrowheads. We are fortunate in finding on our newly acquired property the bony framework of what may well turn out to be the head of a famous Apache warrior."

Ben dug Pete in the ribs. "Watch close now."

Elwin, holding the skull aloft, began an imaginative restoration. "This head, as you can see, is well formed and somewhat broad. With high cheekbones, it probably set firmly on a short, muscular neck." Elwin's finger described substance where the hole came in the middle of bone. "Picture a straight nose," he said, "black eyes blazing with fire and energy... strong jaws and firmly-closed lips...." Elwin clenched and re-clenched his teeth to demonstrate. "See the coarse, thick black hair, but realize the sparse beards that...."

Ben whispered in Pete's ear, "Does that look like the head of a dead Injun to you?"

"Hell, I don't know."

Clasping the skull to his chest, Elwin described a wide arc with his right arm. "They terrorized the Southwest, the Western plains, and Texas."

Ben blurted, "Pete, for Chri'sake, where did they bury old man Johnson?"

Pete glanced again at the skull, then back to the quivering cowboy. "Now wait. How long...you don't think? Let's count. Let's see...he's been dead years and years. Good Lord, where did they bury old man Johnson?"

"Shush. Not so loud."

Pete grasped Ben's arm and they started the slow, ducking, dodging trip back through the crowd to the kitchen. There were people there too.

"Here," ordered Pete, "into the pantry. Now, where did that skull come from?"

"I don't know. Honest. I've just been helpin'. I dug into gopher holes, old mine shafts, shallow wells, along the irrigatin' ditch, in the thicket, everywhere. Elwin must have dug up old man—I mean, I don't know if that's an Injun or not."

Ben held out both hands, palms upward. "Look at my blisters."

Pete rubbed his chin. "You've had rope burns, but I never saw shovel blisters on *your* hands before."

"You never saw me chasin' a skittish redhead before." Ben licked his left palm. "And for all the good these blisters has done me, I may as well have 'em on my ass."

The pantry door burst open and Gladys, talking over her shoulder to a caterer, entered saying, "It takes so many glasses, we'll need to replenish—" She stopped, smiled at Ben and said, "Oh, here you are. A Mr. Gonzalez is looking for you."

Buzzard Ben stepped forward eagerly, obviously hoping to squeeze through the doorway with Mrs. Luscomb.

Gladys backed away, catching the caterer off balance and setting him sprawling on the tile floor.

She is fast, marvelled Pete, leaving the pantry and confusion behind. The living area was more clogged with guests than when he had been there before. He skirted a table and eased past the fireplace.

Elwin held his small audience enthralled with lurid tales of the past. "The battle now opened again on both sides and continued. Hostile Apaches, armed with spears, bows and arrows...." Half an hour passed.

Unnoticed, Pete slipped outside and mopped his

forehead with the back of his arm. Seeing Buzzard Ben and Gonzalez in deep conversation at the end of the table, he walked over. As he reached them the two men raised their cups, clinked rims together and called, "*Tiswin!*" They drank deeply.

Ben wiped his sleeve across his lips. "I'll bet the Apaches would never of been satisfied with *Tiswin* after they tasted this stuff of Elwin's."

Gonzalez, the tall Mexican who owned a ranch in the hills on south of Buzzard Ben's outfit, smoothed his black moustache and said, "'Allo, Pete."

Pete nodded as he edged closer to Ben. "Where in hell did you get those cups you're tossing around?"

"Found 'em in the house. Run out of anythin' to drink out of, so I went in and brought out a armload from that cupboard in the front room."

"Oh, God. You got hold of Gladys's bone china."

"How do you know?"

"Fred and I drove some of Luscombs' steers home. We were here the day the china arrived from back east. Elwin dropped the end of the crate, and Gladys put on a bigger show than a mother quail protecting her nest."

Gonzalez handed his cup to Pete. "I think I go now."

Pete, holding the fragile white china in both hands, stared at Ben. "How many of these did you bring out?"

"Alls I could stack on my arm. Hell, I didn't count 'em."

Pete set his cup inside the one Ben was cradling in shaking fingertips. "You'd damn sure better get them back into the house before Gladys sees you, or you'll be on her 'S' list from now on."

"Help. I need help."

"Don't look at me."

"Where's Fred?"

Pete shrugged and walked off, saying over his shoulder, "I don't know where any of my family is."

"At least find Gladys," Ben begged, "and find out how much of this stuff she had. I've put in too much time with her to break my stick now."

Five minutes later Pete found Gladys in the kitchen.

"Mrs. Luscomb?" he asked, knowing he was interrupting.

Gladys was busy giving instructions to a caterer, trying to push two quarreling cowboys outside, and smooth her up-swept hairdo.

"Mrs. Luscomb," insisted Pete, "how many cups did you say there are in that bone china set of yours?"

"Twenty-seven," she answered, stepping adroitly between the tall cowboys and managing to lead one toward the back door.

Pete followed and walked around the east side of the house rather than attempt the trip back through. Some five-year-old boys had the area in the patio almost blocked off with overturned lawn chairs and potted plants. "Hi, Mr. Moore," called the freckled kid. "Want to play hide-and-go-seek?"

"I am playing. And I'm it."

By the time he climbed his way around to the front of the house again, Ben was gone. Fred met him saying, "We reshelved twenty-six cups plus an extra saucer."

"That's right. One more cup to hunt, but it's not up to us. Find your mother and let's go home."

"I promised Ben I'd help. Besides, I doubt if you'll get Mother home so soon. She didn't know the punch was spiked and is kicking up her heels."

"Where is she?"

"With the girls. They encourage her to get out and relax once in a while. I think you ought to tell her to take it easy with the punch, though."

"Messing around with dudes," stormed Pete, "is like messing around with skunks. First thing you know, you smell as bad as they do." He returned to the living room in search of his wife.

Elwin, still standing by the fireplace, had finished his tales of the primitive Apache and was up to activities during the Civil War. "...too shrewd for the white man," he said, "and their hiding places too rough and remote for soldier or civilian to attack with success. There were times, however," he continued, "when the Indians were taken by surprise and suffered heavy losses. In the year eighteen-sixty-four on the fifteenth of March, a large band of redskins ran a herd from Cow Springs. Captain Witlock went in pursuit...."

Pete could see neither his wife nor any of his daughters. He walked on to the kitchen. There was Pearl, standing in the middle of the floor, mimicking Elwin to the extreme delight of several local folk. She had the remaining bone china cup in her hand. Holding it high, she said, "Note strong Apache features. Imagine high cheekbones...."

Buzzard Ben, eyes following the waving cup like a coyote stalking a rabbit, inched closer.

Gladys, blue eyes wide and horrified, stood behind him.

Pete elbowed his way to his wife. "Enough, Pearl," he spoke softly, reaching for the cup.

"No, no, no, no, no," she answered playfully. "Haven't 'splained about how eyes blazed with fieeeeeerce energy."

"Please, Pearl. Careful. Don't drop—"

Kitchen noises stopped as the white cup flew into the air and made two slow revolutions.

Gladys gasped.

Buzzard Ben turned and covered his ears.

Pete reached up, juggled the china and pulled it safe to his chest.

People cheered when Pete handed Gladys the piece from her precious collection. Voices rose and conversation began.

As the crowd melted away, Ben turned and leaned speechless against the sink.

Gladys, smiling again, took over as hostess and led the last of the group into the living room. "We all need food. Do try some of these little watercress sandwiches. Mrs. Moore?" But Pearl had already ducked her head and slipped out of sight.

Elwin and his audience were gone. Children came in to continue their game of hide-and-go-seek. Gladys closed glass doors on her bone china collection and began pulling little boys from behind heavy red draperies and little girls from under bamboo furniture. She asked Pete, "Where is your wife? I want to show her the rest of the house. It's always been my dream to buy an authentic old adobe, re-do it, and—you know—let myself go."

To her retreating back Pete mumbled, "The Old Johnson Place could be a nice addition to my outfit. Now it is ruined by a damned useless house." His feet were killing him. He hobbled into the yard and squatted alone at the back of the house. Flies buzzed. Heat waves forced extra sweat through the underarms of his blue denim shirt. Unable to rest, he stood and began to prowl.

Half an hour later Pete found his eldest daughter and gave her instructions to find Pearl and take her home. Then he began hunting for Fred.

Inside the house he saw Gladys losing ground in her attempt to quiet all children. "Don't try to corral them in here," Pete suggested. "Take them outside and loose herd them awhile."

"It *is* after sundown." Gladys seemed relieved. "Really time to choose partners for square dancing. Outside everybody."

Her smile was growing strained, and her pink net skirt sagged at the hem where somebody had stepped on it. "I'll have Elwin turn on flood lights and connect the public address system for dancing."

Pete didn't shoo. He sat on the couch and rested his aching feet on a square hassock.

Gladys gave her living room a quick appraisal. Catching her eye, Pete began speaking apologetically. "Mrs. Luscomb, I hope you didn't mind Pearl making fun of Elwin. It's just that she's part Apache herself."

"Your wife?"

"Most anybody whose family has lived along this river in Arizona for three generations has some Indian blood on one side or the other."

Gladys's wan smile faded completely. "Dear me. I'm afraid we have committed a *faux pas*. I'm sure Elwin has no idea...your daughters and handsome son..." She faltered, stroked her hair and added, "I *am* so sorry. I'll tell Elwin." She hurried out the front door.

Pete leaned back on the couch and hoped Fred would come hunting for him. "I can't do much more sashaying afoot," he mumbled, "and I still have that quarter mile walk out to the truck."

From the side door, Gonzalez entered the darkening living room. "*Elena?*" he called softly, giving the Spanish accent to the name Helen.

"Lost your woman?"

"You see her, no?"

"No."

"I fear a storm. It is good we go before too much water fall in the hills."

74

"Let her rip," said Pete, stretching on the couch.

A clap of thunder rolled ominously, drowning out for half a minute the sounds of music and laughter outdoors.

"I 'urry now," insisted Gonzalez.

Pete leaped up. "I wonder why Fred didn't warn me. I've got to get that truck three miles down the road and across the river before a flood comes rolling down."

Elwin's voice came from the hall. "Wait, Helen, I'll find the light switch...there."

The large living room was suddenly illuminated by the indirect lighting. Elwin walked into the middle area. He held a lovely young woman by the arm. She was fair, blond hair reaching below her waist.

Gonzalez's black eyes were two angry slits in his dark face. After a terse 'thank you-goodbye,' he departed with his wife.

While Pete watched the scene he was mentally kicking himself for feeling he had to stay at the party until he had personally checked out every member of his family.

Elwin rubbed his finger tips back and forth across his silver belt buckle. "What local social error did I commit now?"

"Gonzalez is jealous is all."

"Because I was guiding the young woman?"

"You had a grip on her arm. That's enough to throw Gonzalez."

Elwin blinked, "I say, I've made another mistake. I told Fred I saw you get in the car with Pearl."

Pete charged the door. "Fred's not dancing? He's gone?"

Gladys tried to block his way. "Oh, dear," she protested, "everybody is leaving at once."

There was complete confusion as motors started, horses neighed, people called, and thunder rumbled.

Pete cleared the door and ran across the yard yelling, "Gonzalez, wait. Give me a ride."

Lightning highlighted the whole range of southern mountains. A split second later came the onslaught, as the storm broke.

Unmindful of his aching feet, Pete hurried through the gate hoping to find a car going west. He was too late. When the next thunder-rumbling thinned, he heard the crashing sound of rolling water. Flood from the east had already hit the San Pedro River.

Pete trudged back toward the house. He was wet to the skin.

Cupping his hands around his mouth, he turned toward his headquarters and yelled as though he expected his family to hear.

"Damn it to hell, I called it, didn't I? I'm dude trapped."

Marooned

At eight o'clock the evening the electrical storm stopped; a dozen people remained at The Wickiup. All were Tucson friends with the exception of Pete and Ben.

As though on signal, Elwin threw open the front door. Cool moist air swept into the living room. Two couples, standing near the fireplace, raised their noses, sniffed, and sighed.

"Ah, yes, heavenly," croaked a heavy-jowled woman.

Gladys peered into the dusk. "My, I'm surprised it isn't dark yet."

Buzzard Ben, poking his head between Elwin and Gladys, said, "No, but in a couple of hours it'll be blacker than the insides of a cow."

A swarm of insects whipped through the open door and hovered in the center of the room.

"What's that?" asked Elwin, slamming the door.

"A heavy screen ain't very pretty," remarked Ben, "but you sure ought to put one on if you expect to keep mosquitoes 'n flies from eatin' you alive."

Gladys ran to the kitchen and returned carrying a spray gun. Guests failed to shoo the flying ants outside. More were finding their way in.

"Turn off the lights," Pete suggested.

Switches snapped off. Gladys pumped the spray gun.

"Duck ever'body," warned Ben.

"Oh, oh, oh," came the voice of the woman with the deep, frog-like voice. "They're in my hair."

Gladys must have turned the spray gun in the direction of pleading tones, because another series of "no, no, nos" followed.

"Why don'cha duck?" Ben sounded exasperated. "Like this."

A splintering crash followed his words.

"My china!" screamed Gladys. "Elwin, turn on the lights."

After some fumbling, Elwin flipped the hall switch.

Gladys lowered the spray gun and raised her wide bosom in a sigh of relief. Bone china was safe, but a three-way lamp was on the floor in front of the couch. Its turquoise-colored shade rocked and settled on the throw rug. Bulbs and glass reflector lay broken on the red concrete.

Ben sat on the floor trying to untangle the cord from around his boot heels. He grinned sheepishly. "A good half-hitch'll sure hold."

Sputtering and brushing at insects, people ran for the bathrooms and kitchen.

Elwin's tall body sagged against the wide door frame, as he surveyed the waxy, orange-colored ants that were wriggling and dying.

Pete put his muddy boots on the floor and said to Ben, "Get a broom, cowboy."

Half an hour later the Luscomb home neared normalcy. Gladys, relaxed and reposed in lavender

78

lounging pajamas, was a smiling hostess again. "We may as well all go to bed. I believe I can find sleeping places for everyone."

Buzzard Ben asked, "What have you lined up for me?"

Gladys motioned to the sofa.

"There?" Ben eyed the soft cushions and shrugged. "I'll bet I won't be able to feel myself restin'."

Pete stuffed out his cigarette against an Indian arrowhead mounted in a copper ashtray and settled back on a platform rocker. "I'm staying right here."

Gladys and Elwin turned off lights and led their friends down the hall toward bedrooms.

"Uncover the old well, dear," Gladys instructed her husband. "The children have all gone now."

Sounds of laughing and joking floated up the hall.

Ben flounced on the couch. "I've herded steers till they bedded down with less trouble than Gladys is havin' with her visitors."

Pete reached for another cigarette. "Who ever thought I'd follow my wife to a housewarming and wind up sleeping with dudes and bunch of city folks."

After an undetermined time, Ben pounded the couch with his fist. "Are you asleep, Pete?"

"Hell no."

Ben creaked the springs again. "Whoa bed," he pleaded.

"What's the matter? Couch moving?"

"Ever time I close my eyes, the cushions go to buckin'."

"You drank too much of Elwin's *Tiswin*."

Several minutes later, after moans, groans, and "whoas", there came a thump. "I give up," said Ben, rolling up in a rug on the floor. "I've rode broncs that could take a lesson from this sunfishin' couch."

The house grew quiet. Minutes ticked by. Odor of

mashed ants and fly spray hung in the room. Pete went to the very edge of sleep wondering if Ben realized he was being watched over by the noble spirit peeking through the hollow eye of Elwin's dead Indian on the mantel.

Somewhere around midnight a knock rattled the front door.

Pete roused from sleep. Spitting a dead cigarette from between his lips, he felt his way to the door and opened it. The night was still and black in spite of thousands of twinkling stars. He reached for the light switch. "Is that you, Gonzalez? Where's Helen?"

"*Elena* is 'ere," the Mexican answered, pushing his young wife into the living room. Her long yellow hair hung wet and tangled down her back. She blinked in the sudden glare and twitched her nose like a frightened rabbit.

Gonzalez pointed to the Navajo rug on the floor, as a loud "aazaumph kaguph" sounded from the roll.

Pete closed the door. "Don't mind Ben. His snores sound louder than the roar of a loaded Ford going up a sand wash even when he hasn't been drinking."

"We no go to my rancho," said Gonzalez unnecessarily.

"Any knothead can see that. What did you do, turn around and try to come back?"

"But yes."

Helen shivered and hung onto her husband's arm.

"Well, do like the rest of us and bed down. We'll get out of here come morning."

"*La troca*," said Gonzalez, "is in big arroyo one mile from here only. I wait. I dig. I wait. More water comes soon from the mountains. I think *la troca*...." His hand made a wide, expressive sweep-away gesture, while his eyes searched the room.

"Mr. Luscomb is no mad? He will take tractor and pull, no?"

"Elwin isn't mad about you being jealous of Helen. Hell, he doesn't hold a grudge either. Trouble is he can't drive a tractor, and his hired help passed out this afternoon." Pete added, "Worthless bastards."

Gonzalez touched Pete's shoulder. "You drive?"

Pete looked at the shivering couple. He thought of Gonzalez's new pickup. "Sure," he said, shrugging off his lack of mechanical know-how. "Come on. We'll go around outside to the back bedrooms and hunt for Elwin."

They tapped on three windows and woke groggy-voiced couples before they found Elwin, who mumbled, "Take the tractor."

Pete convinced Gonzalez his wife would be safe where she huddled on an easy chair as far from snoring Ben as possible.

Inside the implement shed Pete climbed onto the padded seat and pressed the starter button. There was no time for grease job or warm-up. Gonzalez climbed aboard with a lantern. The engine roared. "It would ordinarily wake the dead," said Pete, "but it won't bother that household."

With bucks and stops of a balky horse, the machine backed out of the shed. Pete felt tracks bite into soft, rain-sodden earth, as the tractor spun under the ranch sign and rumbled west.

It was less than a mile to the arroyo.

"She's 'ere," cheered the Mexican, flashing light over the pickup's front end.

"High-centered," said Pete, throttling the engine, "but at least you got her turned back to this side of the wash. I wish Fred was here. I'm not too expert on one of these crawler-type tractors. I'd hate to get

81

out there in the middle of two feet of running water and get this heavy equipment in a spin."

Water rolled over the bed of the truck where it tilted into a deep rut. The front end was clear of the main channel and was completely dry. By lantern light the men hitched the chain around the axle and climbed onto the tractor again.

"Here we go!" When Pete let out the clutch all at once, the machine lurched, took up on the chain, strained, threatened to die. He disengaged the clutch. "Hey, Gonzalez, how do you get to a lower gear?"

The Mexican pointed to a floor lever.

Wrong choice. Pete pulled other levers, lucked out and felt more power roar. Again the tractor took up on the chain—jerked strained, jerked...jerked, until the motor died.

"Oh, God," Pete moaned, hitting the starter button. *Buzz, buzz, buzz.* Nothing came alive.

"'Urry," urged Gonzalez, "or *la troca* she gone."

"Hell, I can't hurry. I'm not even started." Pete stamped the starter and wished the job could be done with horse help.

Minutes ticked by. Pete's curses were long, loud, and expressive.

Over and over, the Mexican mouthed, "*Madre Dios.*"

Finally, Pete sighed with resignation. "Looks like she's a goner."

"No, no. Try one time more, *por favor.*" Holding his breath, Pete tried. The engine gasped, caught and purred. The tractor backed and yanked the chain, but the truck refused to budge. "I hope to hell we don't jerk the guts out of something."

After two more tries, he yelled, "Yahoo, I feel her moving."

Gonzalez ground his teeth and leaned forward, as

though his straining would help the tractor pull.

As Pete drove the machine, he looked over his shoulder and watched the truck scrape sand, spew water and bounce over the bank onto the road.

"You save *la troca.*" Gonzalez cheered when Pete throttled down the engine. He tried to hold the lantern and embrace the old cowman at the same time.

"Let's hope so." Pete climbed down, took the lantern and walked to the end of the chain. Flashing the light around, he surveyed the pickup. "You've got half a load of river sand in the bed where water washed."

Gonzalez opened the door, slid under the wheel and stepped on the starter. "She's no start."

"Put her in neutral and I'll pull you to the corral. Maybe the engine will dry out by morning."

It was a slipping, sliding return trip. Pete stopped the tractor under the shed, turned ignition off and walked with his neighbor to the house.

The place was as quiet as when they left. Entering the front door, Pete whispered, "I won't turn on a light. Do you want to sleep on the couch? Don't trip over Ben."

Ben let them know where he was by varying his steady snore with a loud "sarumpth."

"I will find *Elena.*"

"You're going down the hall." Pete's whisper grew louder.

"Helen is over here. Hey, come back. You used to know your way around this house, but Gladys—"

"'Elp!"

"God Almighty. Don't tell me I have to fish a wet Mexican out of a 1868 romantic old well." He turned on the lights.

Gonzalez was draped over the winch, holding on to the rope with the bucket over his head.

Pete stood him on his feet and reached for the bucket.

In a matter of minutes, Luscombs' friends crowded into the hall. There was hubbub in The Wickiup abode.

Like a wet dog, Gonzalez shook himself. *"Madre Dios."* He moaned.

His wife ran to him, sleep veiling her eyes. Her blond hair, partially dry, was a tangled mat.

"Elena!"

Gladys stammered, "Wh..., where did you come from? I'm sure I didn't prepare a bed for you."

Elwin, blinking, stifled a yawn.

Pete asked, "Are we going to try to bed down?"

"No," Gladys answered. "There has been too much excitement. I'll go to the kitchen and whip up scrambled eggs."

"Good," agreed Pete. He let go of the winch and let the bucket drop. "Where is the cover for this man trap?"

"I'm sure we all know about the well now," said Gladys. She took Pete's arm and led him into the kitchen. "Where did the Gonzalez couple come from? I distinctly remember—"

"Showed up about midnight." In hushed, hurried whispers he brought her up to date on the night's activities.

People drifted back to their bedrooms and dressed.

Thirty minutes later Gladys called, "Bacon and eggs in the kitchen everybody, stand-around style."

"I may as well eat breakfast," Pete said to no one in particular. Nobody paid any attention when he added, "It'll be daylight at four o'clock, and I can get out of this damned nest."

For the next two hours people ate, wandered around the rooms and recounted other storms they had weathered. As Pete listened he noticed each story grew more colorful. When he heard about hailstones the size of tennis balls, he mumbled, "First liar hasn't got a chance."

Everyone ignored Buzzard Ben, who snored peacefully inside the rolled rug by the sofa.

At three in the morning Gladys noticed Pete out in the patio watching for the first paling of the eastern sky. "Won't you join us?" she asked.

"It's light enough to see, and I sure ought to get home. Do you suppose Elwin would loan me a horse? I'll send Fred back with it today, or tomorrow for sure."

"Of course."

"I'll wrangle out of the pasture afoot." In the desire to get away, Pete forgot the misery of aching feet and displeasure about walking anywhere. He heard the river, a quarter mile away. It filled the early morning with an ominous rumbling sound.

It was after four o'clock when he had Elwin's seven horses in the corral closest to the small barn. Most of the men and some women leaned over the fence and watched Pete throw a saddle on Gladys's black horse. He buckled the flank cinch and whispered to Elwin, "There really isn't another one here I'd risk my neck on. I think you own a bunch of has-beens."

Mr. Luscomb's voice sputtered. "Well, now...."

"You'll never gather your cattle this fall if you don't have good horses." Pete's mind raced as he assured himself he was minding his own business, because if Elwin didn't ride sound mounts gathering stock, he'd expect to borrow horses from neighbors.

He mounted, and as he rode out of the corral he said, "Your fancy bulls survived the storm. I hear them bawling for feed."

The Luscombs and two other couples walked across

the mushy ground to watch Pete ford the river. Wet mesquite branches dripped water whenever they were brushed aside.

Riding ahead, Pete saw the river first. He didn't utter a word. He simply sat and stared. In his lifetime he had never seen the San Pedro so full. The reddish-brown, dank-smelling water rolled along at a furious pace, carrying parts of wire fences, tree branches and brush along the crest of the water. A strip of land almost half-acre wide was washed away.

"My spring!" Pete's anguished voice repeated. "My spring! It's gone." He loped Gladys's black horse along the edge of the fields. Irrigating ditch and spring were under water. The fence, ripped from the ground, had washed away, and the river lapped over onto fields all along the strip of bottom land belonging to the Old Johnson Place.

Turning, Pete rode back to where the others stood. There was a babble of voices as everyone spoke at once. Not Pete. He sat quietly watching the crest of the river. One by one the others stopped talking. They stood, watched and listened as though hypnotized by sight and sound of the swollen river. It seemed angry, roaring with an ominous, throbbing beat.

Finally Pete spoke familiarly to his mount. "Are you ready, boy? It's time we hit the swimming water."

Elwin pulled at Pete's stirrup fenders. "I say, you can't possibly think about plunging into that torrent."

"Come back to the house," Gladys pleaded, "and ride home tomorrow."

Friends agreed it would be a foolhardy stunt.

"She's rolling, but she's clearing," Pete said. "I know I can get across if I don't get fouled up in wire and stuff. That's the danger, and I haven't seen anything floating or bobbing out there for ten minutes." He dismounted, unbuckled and stepped out of chaps. Handing them to Elwin, he added, "I won't need to borrow these, thanks."

Still taking his time, Pete unbuckled spurs and pulled off his boots. These he tied behind the saddle.

Tucson friends looked aghast.

"Oh, no," Gladys said. "And what about your clothes?"

"I can swim with them on if I have to. I'm all set now."

Elwin gave up trying to fold sweat-stiffened chaps and held them across one arm. "Why don't you at least roll up your pant legs?"

Pete stuck a stocking foot in the left stirrup. "I'll leave them down so they'll shed the mud."

Pete took one last look at the swollen river, sizing up the rate of flow, the more than two-hundred-yard width, and the shoreline on the opposite bank. "Here is the best crossing, so I'll ride upstream a quarter mile before I start and let the current carry me down."

As planned, he turned his mount into the water obliquely upstream and headed for the other side of the river. Dropping the reins, he let the horse have his head. From a distance behind, he heard faint cheers and pleas, but he paid no attention.

Pointed against the flood, Pete kept his eyes open for floating debris. With the current pushing them, he and the black horse moved along at a fast clip. They were low in the water. Only the horse's head and neck showed above the swirling tide. Reddish-brown flood water, heavy with silt, soaked Pete's trousers and dragged against his thighs. The dank smell was strong to his nostrils. The crashing roar grew louder in his ears.

When the horse started to turn downstream, Pete

cupped his left hand and splashed water against Blacky's left eye to turn him back. He knew if pulled on the bit, Blacky might inhale water and panic.

"Easy, boy," Pete said. "We've almost got it made."

After two more straining pulls, the horse crossed the main channel and began swimming in quieter water.

Minutes later Pete felt the lurch, as his mount's feet touched earth. Picking up the reins, he was careful to let the horse regain his own footing on the slippery bank.

On solid ground, Pete turned and looked across the river. "Blacky," he said to the horse, "those are dudes. They're standing over there shaking their heads and saying what a stupid idiot I am. They come West, build man traps and get themselves in crying scrapes every day without realizing how dumb they are. But let an old cowboy do something he knows how to do and they call him an ignorant sonofabitch."

Pete reined toward home, thinking. *The flood washed away land and spring. It isn't the way I planned it, but Elwin will have to leave now. Without irrigation water for his land, he can't make a crop. There is no way he'll be able to stay.*

Queen Waterway

One evening in September Pete sat on the front porch in his favorite leather chair and blew cigarette rings at mosquitoes outside the screen. Pearl pulled her treadle sewing machine over to the west end of the porch and began mending brush snags in a pair of Levi's.

The Moores sat in companionable silence for several minutes before Pete, not noticing his cigarette was dead between his lips, took a couple of smokeless drags. "Sure good to be home. I'll be glad to saddle up in the morning and start checking around."

"I haven't seen hide nor hair of our neighbors for two weeks," Pearl remarked.

Pete shifted boot heels on the wooden ledge. "I don't suppose Gladys and Elwin will stay on through the winter. Except for a small domestic well, they haven't any water over there since the flood. Too bad they didn't sell out to me when I offered to buy their outfit."

Pearl's feet stopped treadling. She stared at the

western horizon. "Did you ever see a green sky?"

Dropping boots to the floor, Pete sat up. "No. Must be a sign of something." He looked away from the sunset as his keen ears caught the sound of horses' hoofs. "Somebody's coming."

He threw his cigarette out the front door onto the rocky ground.

"It's the Luscombs and they're riding hell for leather as usual. They must be leaving. Tell them I've gone to bed with the chickens."

"Stay with me. They won't be long."

Pete stopped in his tracks. "You don't suppose they sold out to Ben?"

The Luscombs arrived and reined up sharply in a swirl of dust. They checked their horses, rearing them a few feet from the gate.

Pete threw his hands over his eyes. "I can't watch horses treated that way. A dude buys a long bit for leverage so he can handle a horse; then he can't resist turning his mount on a dime and spinning him around like practicing for a shoot-'em-up picture show."

Gladys and Elwin slid to the ground, tied reins to the fence, and rushed polished boots over the bare yard. "Howdy," they said in unison.

Pearl held open the screened door.

"What's the hurry?" asked Pete.

"Another surprise," trilled Gladys. "I'll bet you've wondered what we've been doing since the storm."

Pete answered, "I've been gone. Took Fred back to school. After that, I—"

Interrupting, Elwin announced, "We drilled a well."

"And I'm going to break a bottle of champagne over the engine and really launch her," Gladys added.

Elwin removed his hat and bowed over it. "We want

you and Pearl to come over and share our happiness."

Pete's wrinkled chin sagged, his mouth opened and shut and opened again, but he was unable to utter a word.

Pearl smiled and closed the screened door, after saying, "We'll be glad to come. We'll drive behind you in the Ford."

Walking toward the garage some minutes later, Pete caught another look at the sunset. "Pearl, if I ever see another green sky, I'll remember the night I found out about the Easterners drilling a well. They don't need my spring. I thought they were leaving. Now it seems they might stay all winter."

Twenty minutes later Pete drove into Luscombs' yard at the same time Gladys and Elwin rode up the trail horseback. On beyond the sign over the gate was the new irrigation setup. Pete whistled when he observed the size of the project. Mounted on a concrete slab, the bright-red engine was almost as big as a Ford, the pump itself looking like a knob over the well. A twelve-inch discharge pipe stuck out over a rock-filled sump. Joining pump and engine were four V belts. The whole installation was enclosed with netting wire and covered by a shed.

"This setup will throw enough water to irrigate two-hundred acres," Pete exclaimed, after he walked close for inspection.

"Naturally," agreed Elwin, dismounting.

"More land," Pete whispered to Pearl, standing beside him. "He doesn't know how to take care of the sixty acres he has."

"Shush," Pearl cautioned.

Buzzard Ben leaned around one side of the shed and called, "Hi."

"You were here when I left, Ben," said Elwin. He

glanced around. "Where is the mechanic?"

"Got tired waitin' and left for Tucson. Sure you didn't hear his pickup? Ain't been gone but a few minutes. Said you won't need him no more anyways."

"And the cowboys?"

"Took the truck an' went to town."

"It's not Saturday night," put in Gladys, sliding off her horse.

Ben guffawed. "They didn't care what night it was when they left. They said they was curly, gray wolves and tonight was their night to howl. Yeee-a-hoo!"

Befuddled, Elwin glanced from one face to another.

Ben patted the knob on top of the pump. "Don't worry about Pump Queenie here. She purrs like a petted pussy cat." He pointed to the dampness in the bottom of the ditch leading away from the sump. "The mechanic cranked 'er up an' tried 'er out 'fore he left."

"Then what are we waiting for?" cried Gladys. "I'll run to the house for the champagne while you men turn on the pump again."

"You take the horses to the corral, and let me'n Pete get it," Ben said. "The pump starts easy, Elwin."

Ignoring Ben's suggestion, Gladys linked arms with Pearl.

Still feeling dazed, Pete walked after Ben. "You act like you've helped yourself to the dude's whisky while he was gone."

"No, he locked it up. But me'n the cowboys polished off the bottle of champagne."

"So that's why the boys felt so damn good they went to town. Well, Gladys is ready to break a bottle over the new pump, so what are you going to tell her?"

A few steps from the house Ben turned. "I can tell

her I couldn't sit around here an' think of pourin' joy juice all over a lifeless hunk of metal that can't taste for sour duck apples."

From the irrigation ditch came the steady clink poof; clink poof; clink poof; as Elwin engaged the crank and pulled without success.

Pete said, "Thought you said the pump was easy to start."

"It was easy as hell for the mechanic."

"You better start thinking what to tell Gladys."

Ben stumbled twice, running through the house to the kitchen, Pete right behind.

Picking the empty bottle off the drainboard, Ben filled it with water and tried to replace the cork. "Hell, it's too big. Look how it swelled up. Whittle on it, will you?"

Pete flipped open his pocket knife and pared the cork.

"Hurry up."

"I am. Here."

Ben wriggled the stopper into the neck, and raked the bottle up and down his Levi's to dry it off. "C'mon. We'll get away with this if we work fast...like magic."

Back at the well, Pete glanced at Elwin's red face and stepped over to take crank in hand. He pulled up a couple of times and then, as he did with his smaller engine at home, jiggled the choke valve and checked the key. There was the trouble. Elwin had neglected to turn it to the "on" position.

Ben, brandishing the bottle above his head, danced around. "Get 'er started, Pete, times' awastin' here."

Pete turned the key, pulled up on the crank once, and stepped back. The engine roared, drowning all small sounds with its steady beat. Clear water streamed from the discharge pipe.

Gladys let go Pearl's arm, ran forward, and called

out, "Champagne."

"Here!" yelled Ben, handing her the bottle of water. She ran to the pump. "Where should I hit it?"

Because of the engine's roar, everyone made motions to different places on the setup.

Standing on the concrete platform, Gladys reached as high as she could and brought the bottle straight down from overhead. There came a splintering smack as the glass hit metal. "I name you Queen Waterway," Gladys shouted over the din. "You are successfully launched."

Almost immediately came a coughing from the engine of the new pump installation.

"Elwin, do something," Gladys pleaded.

Ben laughed. "Ain't nothin' to do. You wet the spark plugs."

The engine sputtered once more and quit.

Elwin looked like a man whose child has refused to show off for company. "I say, we all know it works. Shall we go to the house and drink a toast?"

"Thanks," said Pete, but I have to hurry home. I promised my wife I'd help move the chickens onto the new roost Fred built."

Gladys reached for Pearl's hand. "Don't hurry off. Before you go, you must come out and see *my* chickens."

"All right, but let's unsaddle and feed your horses first."

Elwin said, "Show her the other animals you purchased for the sake of atmosphere."

At that moment the moon showed at the tops of the eastern mountains.

Pete, against his better judgment, went to the house with Ben and Elwin. "Mr. Luscomb, you've enough lawn between the gate and the front door to pasture two saddle horses."

Elwin reached for the door knob. "Beautiful, isn't it?"

The men went inside and sat in the living room. Elwin opened the doors of a cabinet and unlocked the bar. "I'm glad you men approve of my pump and well. It's the best money can buy. Cost me six thousand, counting the ditch work."

Ben whistled. "I'd have to mortgage."

"I understand most of these Western ranches are mortgaged," interrupted Elwin.

"Hell, yes," said Pete, his neck swelling. "We start out on a shoestring, borrow money on our cattle to expand our holdings. When we get that paid for, we borrow more to pay for our improvements."

"Unless we get a bad year," Ben elaborated, "then we're a couple years makin' that up."

Elwin, pouring expertly from a pinch bottle, said, "Don't you find that method rather slow? Aren't interest payments cutting into your profits?"

Pete shuffled his boots on the Navajo rug. "Sure it eats into the profit, but it's slow progress. We're growing all the time. If we didn't figure we had a chance, we'd sell out and put our money in the bank."

Elwin picked up the tray of drinks. "I'm spending a great deal of money here, but I enjoy doing it." He shrugged, "All excess...when you consider taxes...."

"No thanks," said Pete, shaking his head.

After Ben accepted a glass, Elwin set the tray on the coffee table and turned to Pete. "Don't you drink at all?"

"Not at all. Found out a long time ago I can't handle it."

Ben downed his Scotch in quick gulps and reached

for the third glass.

The genial host leaned back in his platform rocker and smiled. "Have any more of my steers strayed onto your range, Pete?"

"Yep."

Ben added, "Anyways they're steers now."

Pete, deciding he had been polite long enough, stood up, congratulated Elwin as the owner of Queen Waterway and added, "After I corral my wife, we'll head for home."

"I'll stick around for awhile," Ben said between sips.

Outside, Pete met Gladys and Pearl in the patio. More goodbyes were exchanged in the moonlight.

The Moores arrived home in half the time it took them to drive to Luscombs' headquarters. There was no conversation during the trip. Pete drove pell-mell over the rutty country road, while Pearl, pressing both feet against the floor, held onto the dashboard. Her salt-and-pepper hair came unpinned, and the ends whipped the air almost a yard behind her head.

After Pete wheeled the Ford into the old board garage, they climbed out.

Pearl's words were non-judgmental and spoken softly. "That was a quick ride."

Pete slammed the garage doors. "It is also the last ride over there."

Pearl began coiling her hair. "Luscombs really put in a big pump while they were about it."

"About three times too big. Elwin has over-expanded the Old Johnson Place until it's impossible for the production on the outfit ever to pay for the improvements...plus that awful house."

The couple walked side-by-side across the rocky yard.

Pete's voice quavered. "Let's turn in right after

chores and forget new neighbors. I admit I'll never be able to buy the Old Johnson Place for Fred."

"Don't worry about our son."

They entered the dark house. Meowing cats welcomed them.

"All right," Pete agreed. "The dudes are off limits as far as I'm concerned. I'll manage to stay out of their way completely."

"I'm not sure you can."

"Watch me!"

Wild Horse Chase

On a crisp morning in November Pete left ranch headquarters.

Riding his horse through frost-nipped mesquite brush, all his senses were alert for sounds of cattle moving in the underbrush—the touch of wind, smell of salt cedars and willow trees, and feel of the horse between his legs. Not far from his house, he stopped, leaned over saddle horn and smoked a cigarette while he watched the trickle of water flowing like a slow-moving salamander through dry, riverbed sand.

"No half measures about the old San Pedro," he mumbled. "She's either up or down. When she's up, she's hell; when she's down, nothing."

Before crossing the river he rode upstream along the east side. Near the middle of the thicket he found a half dozen of his dude neighbor's big steers. "Head the other way, you damned sonsabitches," he shouted.

A call of "Howdy," came from the brush.

Pete paused and listened.

"I say," came the voice again, accompanied this time

by loud popping and crackling of twigs.

Pete smothered a whole mouthful of curses and tried to head off the steers.

With the air of a gladiator, Elwin Luscomb rode his prancing horse past the steers and up to his closest neighbor. Grinning broadly, the dude seemed oblivious to Pete's motions and signs concerning the steers. "How do you like my new horse?" he called. The animal fidgeted, whinnied and, stepping high, moved sideways.

"Can't you see I'm trying to circle these steers of yours?"

"In due time," said Elwin. "Stop now and tell me what you think of my mount. After all, man, you are the one who suggested I purchase some cow ponies. I sold those old ones I had—with the exception of Gladys's black. Cinnamon, here, is only one of six." He stroked and patted golden mane. "I purchased the best money can buy."

"Good God! If the others are like this hot-blooded sorrel, you've bought yourself a half-dozen, quarter-type race horses."

"They're bred to run, but they are also trained as work animals."

"All right," said Pete, reining his heavier boned, brown horse in a neat, tight circle, "let's work him out. We'll drop back to the trail, circle your steers and then see if we can drive them across river onto your place."

Elwin seemed overjoyed at being included in the old cowman's plans. He dug his spurs into Cinnamon's flanks. The small, light-boned horse jumped straight up into the air and came down, legs planted wide and trembling.

Pete leaned down and straightened a pant leg while he pretended not to notice while Elwin got Cinnamon under control. After much urging, the horse finally took a few mincing steps after Pete's well-behaved mount and lagged about fifty paces behind as the two riders rode through the brush.

Pete circled six steers bunched near the trail. When the animals began moving toward the river, Pete saw one duck. "Give him air...he'll come back."

But Elwin had already jerked on reins. Cinnamon planted front feet, kicked up his hind feet, and turned his back to the steer.

"Well-trained," snorted Pete. "If there's one thing I can't stand it's a goddamned horse that sets on his front feet and turns with his ass."

The steer ducked into the underbrush out of sight. Pete held his position in order to keep the other five from following.

Elwin, his back to the bunch, tried unsuccessfully to turn his horse. Cinnamon balked and refused to budge.

Pete urged his horse forward easily and began herding the steers up the trail. Elwin, flapping the reins and rocking in the saddle, was left behind. Pete looked over his shoulder and asked his mount, "What does the damn fool think he riding now, a hobby horse?"

Suddenly the little sorrel reared, whirled and bolted. Eyes wild, Cinnamon charged toward Pete at full gallop.

Elwin made a grab for his hat and dropped the reins.

The steers quit the trail and dodged—three going east and two going west into the brush.

Pete rode off the trail a couple of paces toward the river bank.

Hoofs pounding wildly, Cinnamon raced up the open trail. Elwin stayed in the saddle by gripping the horn with both hands. Pete rode along behind.

Three hundred yards up the trail Cinnamon turned, galloped under a low mesquite limb and stopped. The heavy branch caught Elwin under the ribs and jerked him off.

Seconds later Pete dismounted. With easy, fluid motions he tied both horses. Bending over the supine Easterner he thought if a damned dude could get sense knocked *into* him as easy as he can get wind knocked *out* of him, the sonofabitch might learn to be a cowboy.

Elwin sat up and shook his head.

Pete untied his own horse. "I'll ride back and get your hat."

By the time he returned, Elwin had regained both dignity and breath. "I can't understand what prompted Cinnamon to react in such a manner," he said, standing alongside the docile, quieted horse and stroking his golden mane.

"He just acted like he was taught to act. He thought you wanted him to run a race and he did. He's fast, too. In our local races, I'll bet he'll beat anything we've got for the first three-hundred-fifty yards."

Elwin shook his head sadly. "We lost the steers, and I am disappointed in Cinnamon's showing."

"Don't be disappointed in this little horse. He'll do all right if you keep him on the track and out of a brush thicket."

Elwin glowered. "I paid thousands of dollars for six cow horses, not race horses."

"Then you'd better get your money out of them and buy some horses that aren't so hot-blooded—ones that have more bone to them and feet that can stand the rocks."

Elwin mounted his beautiful, trim horse and reined onto the trail. Cinnamon, head erect, nostrils quivering, responded eagerly. Without a backward glance or a word of parting, the dude rode up the trail. Cinnamon cut a zigzag path as he pranced a few steps forward and then danced sideways.

Pete turned and rode toward home, shaking his head. He started to call the Easterner a poor damned fool but found himself applauding Elwin for being so gutsy.

First day of December Pete rode up the west side of the river near the Old Johnson Place—he was damned if he'd call it Luscombs' Wickiup—to where his spring bubbled up through sand. After August's flood water ran off and the river returned to its normal flow, underground water again found its way to the surface. But the spring was now eight feet below the level of the land, not practical for irrigating fields. The Luscombs didn't need it any more, and the spring water was too far from Pete's land to use even if he installed a pump to lift the water over the bank.

Sitting horseback and watching clear water bubble through the sand and flow uselessly downstream, Pete planned, letting his mind wander. *I'll build a concrete curb around the stream when Fred comes home. Fred's good with cement...a hell of a good son.*

"Whatcha doin? Still moanin' 'bout havin' your goddamned spring washed away?"

"Hello, Ben. No, you old buzzard, you know I don't moan about weather. I was figuring how I could use my spring for a water trough. That way I wouldn't have to fix a float valve."

"Then you'll probably be interested in Elwin's proposition."

"This spring isn't for trade. The water is mine."

"Elwin don't want to buy it. Gladys wants watercress, so they was wonderin' if they put up the material would you supply the labor and then build a little protection of concrete 'round the spring with a dirt fill below."

"So Gladys can have fresh watercress?"

"Sure. An' if I was you I'd take him up on his idea. You ain't got nothin' to lose. Fred'll do the work, the Luscombs'll buy cement an' wood for the forms, an' you'll have a cattle trough free."

"There's nothing that's free. You know damn well if I agree to any such scheme, the spring would probably be fenced off so my cattle wouldn't trample dude watercress. Goddammit, why don't they plant watercress below the sump of their own new setup?"

"Oh, they got a mint bed there...besides, the water flows too fast for watercress, an' besides the ditch goes dry when they're not irrigatin', an' the stuff'd die out, an'—now wait, before you ride off in a huff—hell, I know you don't give a rat's ass, but Elwin wants me to ask you if you want to go on a wild horse chase."

"After being around Easterners, I wind up feeling like I've been on a wild goose chase."

"I said *horse,* not goose."

At the sound of the stressed word Pete whirled. "Is Elwin going to put on a race with those fancy horses he bought?"

"Oh, hell no. They're gone. One named Cinnamon throwed Gladys last Sunday. Then Elwin went to Tucson, got him a truck, loaded up all six an' took 'em to the auction. Man, he sure took a ass reamin'. He lost more money in two weeks than I could spend in a year."

"What are they riding over there?"

"That black of Gladys's and one I traded 'em."

Pete laughed. "I'll bet you got rid of that jugheaded colt that couldn't spread his own poop with a rake tied to his tail."

Ben looked down his nose. "Anyway, they're goin' up in those flats between Black Mountain an' the high plateaus an' catch some wild horses."

"God Almighty, who put them up to that hare-brained scheme?"

Ben didn't look up. "Well, I guess I let it slip that there was unbranded horses runnin' loose in the south hills." He coughed and slipped his calloused hands along leather reins.

"They can't ride those pestle-tails. They're nothing but a bunch of inbred, poor-to-start-with, no-account, worthless—they are not broke saddle horses."

"Aw, think of the fun they'll have chasin' 'em, an' they just might accidental catch a couple."

"There's more chance that Elwin will roll his horse off one of those rock ledges and break his goddamn neck," Pete said.

"Let him kill hisself," Ben gloated. "The only thing that would make that redheaded wife of his look better to me would for her to be a widow."

Leaning over the saddle horn, Pete squinted his eyes. "Elwin damn sure should have kept his race horses to go wild horse chasing. By the way, you aren't planning to ruin one of your mounts loping after those broomtails?"

"Not me. I'm goin' to be settin' at the foot of the mountain real comfortable with a pair of field glasses an' a movin' pitcher machine. Gladys wants action shots of her adrivin' the herd down a sand wash."

Pete groaned. "Go ahead, but I can't sit here and listen to how you've roped those dumb Easterners into thinking they can pull off such a crazy stunt." He turned away from the spring and started toward the river crossing.

"I'll tell Elwin," called Ben, "that you don't want to

join him on his wild horse chase."

"You could have told him that when he asked you," Pete called back.

Before dawn, five days later, Pete drove two new bulls into the foothills. He had blissfully forgotten about the wild horse chase and his visit with Ben until he crossed a mesa, skirted a mesquite thicket and saw him sitting on a rock in the middle of a sand wash.

Ben was not alone. The Luscombs, astride horses, were there. Nearby was a tripod, two suitcases and several boxes.

Without hesitation Pete changed plans. He chose not to drive bulls up that particular wash. He turned west, deciding to cross two ridges and leave the bulls half way up another cut between hills. Pulling his hat brim low on his forehead, he muttered, "I won't get mixed up with any dudes running horses today or any other day. I'll leave the bulls as quick as I can and ride to the windmill on the south end of my place and see how the triggers on my catch gates are working."

Before Pete had the bulls turned, Gladys and Elwin overtook him at full gallop. He wondered why they didn't wake up and realize he wanted to keep out of their way.

"Yoo hoo," hailed Gladys, rearing her black horse to a sudden stop. "Mr. Moore, if I didn't know you better, I might think you are avoiding us."

Elwin pulled up alongside his wife. "I say, do come along. We're short-handed."

Pete stopped. "Are you and Gladys planning to chase wild horses alone?"

"No," said Elwin. "Our two cowboys and a local

Mexican boy are at this time high on the plateau, where they camped last night in order to obtain and keep the advantage of our quarry."

"Honestly," began Gladys, filling her lungs with crisp December air. "I am constantly amazed at how natives take things for granted. It must take an Easterner to appreciate Indian lore and beautiful, untamed horses."

"We appreciate them. Not only that, we have sense enough to leave them alone."

Gladys laughed. "No one can leave such gorgeous creatures alone once they really observe them." She turned her mount and started back toward Ben.

"You've actually seen the wild horses?" called Pete.

"Naturally. Elwin found them in binoculars three days ago, didn't you, dear? They were running along the tops of the ridges."

Pete, again flanked by the Luscombs, returned to the sand wash. He forgot all about asking Ben to lend him some cigarette makings, when he saw his neighbor beside a pile of rocks unpacking bags and boxes at the base of a heavy-trunked cottonwood tree. Field glasses hung from a leather thong around his neck.

"Hi, Pete," Ben said. "Take a look at all this stuff." He pointed to a small, square suitcase. Attached to it was a hundred-foot cord and microphone. "We even got a wire recorder. When the horses gallop down the sand wash, I'll set the gadget here." He placed the microphone stand on a big rock out away from his hiding place. "That ought to catch the hoofbeats real good." He gave a high-pitched imitation of a horse whinny and slapped his thighs, making the sound of a fast-galloping horse. "Won't that be somethin' to go with the pitcher?" He opened another case that held a movie machine and a stack of reels. Reaching up and twisting his hat back to front and well up on scraggly hair, he made cranking motions with his right arm. "Cant'cha see me grindin' away like a big movie man?" He dropped his arm and spun on a boot heel. "See? I even figgered 'bout the sun. Now, when horses come chargin' toward the river down this narrow wash, it ought to be 'bout mid-afternoon give or take a little." He swung his index finger across the sky to a point over the tops of southwest hills. "The sun'll be there. Gladys wants to catch highlights bouncin' off the horse's coats."

Pete, who had done nothing but stare openmouthed at Ben, glanced at Gladys. She nodded with obvious approval.

Elwin scanned the tops of hills with binoculars. "We may catch a glimpse of them any time. The sun is up, and the chase is on."

Gladys moistened lips with the tip of her tongue. "Elwin, are you sure I can handle the snare alone?"

"You'll have to, my dear." He swept tops of the ridges with binoculars. "I'll be busy at the trap half mile farther up the trail."

"What trap?" snapped Pete, having horrible visions of himself disappearing into a dude-dug hole.

Elwin lowered field glasses and smirked at Pete. "Don't tell me a born Westerner like yourself never put rope snares on the trail. My dear man, it's a trick almost as old as the West."

Gladys dropped both reins in order to draw Pete a picture with her hands. "You simply take a lariat and make a big loop and lay it opened on the trail where the horse will have to step. Then you hide behind a rock and pull up on the rope when the horse steps in the loop." Her laugh sounded joyful. "Haven't you ever done that?"

107

Pete glanced at Ben, but Ben was busy setting up his movie equipment. "No," answered Pete. "My rope is tied to my saddle horn, and the loop is twirling around over my head."

Elwin patted his lariat, coiled and neatly tied to saddle horn. "We have our ropes, too, you know."

Gladys laughed. "This is sheer delight. Oh, we're going to do everything. We're going to chase, rope, and snare." She motioned toward Buzzard Ben. "He'll take pictures and record."

Gathering her reins, she sighed and finished more slowly, "When the rest of the horses run past us, we'll herd them up the trail and corral them at our ranch, The Wickiup."

"You see, we don't expect a one-hundred-percent catch," commented Elwin, "however, there must have been twenty in the bunch I saw three days ago." He raised binoculars again. "I wonder where the cowboys are? We'll not wait any longer. Are you positive you don't want to ride along, Pete?"

"No thanks. You won't catch me ruining a good horse chasing after worthless mountain ponies."

"Now Mr. Moore," Gladys chided, "we're just going hunting."

In Pete's opinion the only way Luscombs would have a successful hunt would be with .30-30 rifles. Without looking at Ben, he tipped his Stetson. "Well, good luck." Turning his mount, he jogged off down the sand wash. His thoughts were negative, very negative.

After finding his two new bulls and relocating them, he rode the range all day alone. It was almost sundown, when he unsaddled and fed his horse. Odors of food cooking filled the air. He raised his head like a coyote catching the scent of a rabbit. He took another deep breath, figuring Pearl had gone to the Mexican's place and traded eggs for red chili peppers.

He stepped around to the side of the old adobe house where Fred had added a wash basin and a stall shower during one of his trips home from college. His wife stood on the front porch. After greeting her, he said, "Let's eat. Maybe after I get my belly full, I'll be able to forget dudes altogether."

Pearl stepped out the screened door. "What happened today?"

"I'll tell you later." Before he entered the house, he heard voices coming up the road.

Minutes later, a party of four trudged into sight.

"I knew it," Pete said. "Did you ever see a more pitiful sight than two drunk cowboys and a pair of dudes single-footing home half-dragging their saddles?"

"Elwin is limping," Pearl said. "I hope he's all right."

"And Gladys looks like she snared herself or got caught in Elwin's trap, but they'll bounce back. Those Eastern neighbors of ours have more lives than we have cats."

"Why are they afoot?"

"I don't know. Ben likes to 'job' greenhorns. Maybe he sold them on another harebrained idea for catching wild horses."

"So that's what they were trying to do."

"The chase is over without a single catch. Right now it looks like the only thing caught in the loop is me."

"Shall I ask them in?"

"No, they're not interested in food or visiting now. After I help them put saddles in the barn, I'll fire up the Ford and drive the poor suckers the rest of the way home."

Six Easy Lessons

April Fool's Day Pete saddled his buckskin horse. As he buckled the flank cinch, he spoke to his mount. "So you feel like humping up a little this morning, eh, Buck?" Well, it'll be out of you by night. Today we begin roundup." His words were white puffs in the clear air, and the horse's breath was also a vapor cloud, disappearing quickly only to form again.

Stepping into the left stirrup and swinging easily into the saddle, Pete continued, "You're wearing new shoes all around; you've been eating grain for a couple of weeks, and it's spring, Buck, dammit to hell, it's *spring.*"

The old cowman faced the chill wind sweeping down off the snow-capped southern mountains. The horse's hoofs clip-clopped along hard, frost-covered ground. He hunched his shoulders and pulled weathered hat low on forehead. *It won't feel much like spring, though, until the sun starts shining.*

By mid-afternoon the day was warm and bright. Pete had ridden up into the south hills to make arrangements to work with Gonzalez a week. They would gather and sort cattle from both ranches.

Around four o'clock Pete neared home. He took the trail to the east of the mesquite thicket between his headquarters and the Old Johnson Place. He had come out of the river and was proceeding downstream when he heard commotion coming from heavy brush. There was a wild "Ki, yi, yippie, git along little dogies." From the cracking and popping of dry twigs, Pete estimated there were six men working a herd of cattle through the thicket.

He rode out on a sandbar and waited. Loud "Hi-ya, hi-ya" calls continued. He looked up and down the trail for two miles and saw nothing but the close growth of bare-limbed mesquite bushes. "Buck," he asked his mount, "I wonder who is working the river this early, and why?"

He waited a full ten minutes before the riders came into view. There was a last burst of wild yelling. Elwin Luscomb galloped his horse onto the river bank, closely followed by two cowboys. Minutes later, three men Pete had never seen before trotted into sight. They were slapping their leather chaps and shouting at the tops of their lungs, as they joined Elwin and his two cowboys. Elwin's wife galloped from the thicket a quarter of a mile south.

Pete reined up the bank and said to the group, "Well, where are the cattle?"

Elwin scratched his ear and looked over his shoulder. "It would seem we did not drive them from the brush as planned."

Bill and Bart, Elwin's regular hired help, glanced at each other sheepishly and Bill said, "We started out driving a big bunch."

Gladys rode up. "Where in the world did the cat-

111

tle go?"

Seeing Pete she added, "Hello, Mr. Moore. As you see, we've returned for the roundup. We were at our home back east for three whole months. Did you miss us?"

Like a kick in the ass, thought Pete, tipping his hat and chucking his chin.

After introducing his Eastern friend, Elwin said, "I rather imagine we will have to return to the west end and make another attempt to drive the herd."

Gladys reared her black horse. "Then shall we all ride to our Wickiup and talk over roundup plans?"

"Excellent idea, my dear," agreed Elwin, with a broad smile. "It is time for afternoon cocktails."

"Hold up a minute, will you?" Pete asked Elwin, as the others galloped off. He made an effort to hold his temper. "You go 'chousing' around in the brush and we'll have to rope these river cattle to get them shipped out of here. Part of them are mine, and I sure as hell would like to see them gentle enough for a man to handle."

Elwin threw out his chest. "I wish to gather my cattle as well. It is roundup time, I believe?"

"I don't know if you have an idea how we run our roundups around here," said Pete, "but I can tell you in a damn few words you can't work this brushy mountain country, with a river in the middle of it, like you would the plains."

"Harumph." Elwin cleared his throat, his face reddening.

"That's a hell of a good looking horse you're riding."

The dude's face cleared. "Glad you like it." Patting the bay's neck, he said, "Yes, sir, I spent a lot of money, but I have five good, sensible saddle horses. And in time for roundup, eh?"

Pete, openly admiring the horse, said, "He's almost

what we call a blood bay. He's got a good head on him. How's his spirit? Does he take an interest in his work? How old is he?"

"What difference does age make if a horse works well? Ah, yes, about work—if you don't drive the cattle from the thicket, how do you gather them?"

The old cowman sealed his cigarette by first licking tongue up its length and then twisting one end with thumb and forefinger. "In the first place we get together with neighbors and make arrangements to ride a couple of days with each one. I'm going up to Gonzalez's place next week, and we'll work a while on top where some of our cattle mix."

"I say, that does make sense," said Elwin. "Then, since your cattle and mine are in this thicket, when shall we work?"

"We don't work the river till last." He inhaled smoke before continuing. "There's no use to gather the easy ones in April and hold them through till June. We always go after the hard ones first, branding calves and doctoring as we go along."

The Easterner squirmed in the saddle. "Would you think...that is...would I be forcing myself into your established..." Elwin slapped the ends of his reins against his chaps. "May I ride with you and Gonzalez?"

"It's all right with me. Some of your stuff is bound to be on top. Those big steers of yours never did locate very well. They're covering country like mountain goats in a drouth."

"That's great. Now how about a cocktail? We should drink to our return. I propose a toast to this wonderful winter climate."

"No thanks."

"I say, I forgot you don't drink. Don't you hire any men either? I usually see you alone."

113

"I manage to keep a couple of men busy," Pete answered, "but unless my son is home, like during holidays, I prefer to work by myself except in the spring."

"Then it is arranged. I will bring my men and meet you the morning of the seventh. No, that is Sunday. We had better make it the eighth."

"The seventh. During roundup, Sunday is just another day. Meet us at the fork of the road, the turnoff by your ranch sign. I'll be there with my 'boys' at four o'clock."

"Four o'clock in the morning?"

"Sure. We have to meet Gonzalez and top out by sunup."

Elwin twisted polished boots in his stirrups. "That means if our guests stay over Saturday, we will have a party. Great Scot! I won't get any sleep at all."

"Send your company home," suggested Pete under his breath, "and go to be bed with the damn chickens." He waved his hand in parting. His advice was, "Wear a wool sweater under your jacket. We're only three thousand feet here on the river, but we'll be a mile high at Gonzalez's. G'bye."

Riding toward home Pete laughed, thinking of how the idea of being horseback at four o'clock Sunday morning cooled down the Easterner. He wondered if the dude would even show up.

One week later at the appointed hour, Pete and his cowboys waited horseback at the fork of the road. "We'll smoke another cigarette," Pete told them, "but Elwin probably won't come."

Reaching for his tobacco, he added, "I hope to hell he doesn't."

Pete's second smoke was only a half-inch long when

114

he let it die and threw it on the ground. "C'mon, boys, time's awastin'."

From up the road came the faint sounds of rolling stones. "Hold on," Pete cautioned. "I hear something. Maybe it's a cow. Nope, it's a horse—three horses. The dude is late, but he's coming."

Minutes later the sound of galloping hoofs came from the west, followed by a call, "Is that you, Pete?" It was Elwin's voice.

"Hell yes, it's me. Who else are you expecting? Let's move. It'll be a long day."

Cigarettes glowed in the darkness, men's voices mingled, and the horse's hoofs clip-clopped on the frost-covered trail leading away from the road and into the hills.

At sunup the six men met Gonzalez and his men. They trotted on across the mile-high plateau, gathering cattle as they went. Pete looked back at Elwin, who was riding slowly and falling behind. Face drawn, the Easterner hunched against the chill.

"He must have partied last night after all," Pete said to Gonzalez. "Nobody looks that bad unless he's hung over."

Dropping back, he rode alongside his neighbor. "You look done in. Why don't you ride west, cross a couple of hogbacks and wait for us there? We'll swing around with the herd and meet you. You got any matches?"

Elwin nodded.

"Good. Get down with your back to a ledge, stay in the sand wash and build a fire. We'll see you in about two hours."

Elwin didn't need urging. He turned from the wind and rode northwest.

Mid-morning Pete began watching for the Easterner. "He should be along here," he said to Bill and Bart. "You boys ride the other side of the wash. I told him to stay on this side, but he might have ideas of his own."

"I hope he didn't use none of 'em," said Bill.

Pete followed along the east side of the hill for another quarter mile. Raising his head, he sniffed for smoke. No luck. After another quarter mile, he rode up to the top of the nearest hill and looked around, mumbling, "Now where do you suppose that silly dude went? Any ignorant sonofabitch can ride across two ridges and sit his ass down in a damned sand wash."

From Pete's vantage point, he could see along the edge of the ridge, across the canyon westward and back down the sand wash. Fifty head of Hereford cattle plodded along slowly, bawling now and then. Two cowboys rode ahead, checking expertly to slow the pace. Bill and Bart rode west side. Gonzalez and his men were at the rear and on east.

Pete leaned forward and patted his horse. "It'll be one hell of a long day for you, boy, but we'll have to go back to where Elwin left us and track him out."

He found Elwin's trail and followed it—not across two ridges but one, where it turned south up a sand wash.

At four o'clock in the afternoon, when the sun had dropped behind the peaks and the mountains were cooling rapidly, Pete found Elwin. He was huddled in a cave, a prospector's hole, in the side of a hill five miles from where he should have been. His horse was tied outside.

"What in hell are you doing way up here?" Pete asked.

"Waiting for you," answered Elwin through stiff lips.

Pete dismounted. "Why didn't you wait where I told you to?"

"You told me to cross a couple of hogbacks. I say, what is a hogback?"

"A ridge."

Elwin held his head. "I didn't know. Then I became hungry and decided to go back to Gonzalez's headquarters for food while I was waiting."

"You're lucky you didn't spend time with Helen," said Pete, helping the dude to his feet. "If that Mexican knew you were alone with his wife, he'd kill you as easy as he would a treed raccoon."

Elwin shuddered.

"Climb on your horse," Pete ordered, handing him reins.

"Impossible!"

"Nothing is impossible, except making a cowboy out of you," Pete mumbled under his breath. Aloud he said, "Here, up you go."

The rest of the men took care of the cattle, while the Easterner and the old cowboy rode back to Moores' headquarters. It was a slow trip down sand washes out of the hills with Elwin stopping every mile to change his position and ask between gasps how much farther.

At twilight, the two men reached the river crossing south of Pete's place and rode the last short lap north.

Elwin stumbled after Pete entering the ranch house. Hollow-eyed, brush-scratched and putty-colored, he spoke to Pearl. "Have you a drop of whisky in the house?"

Pete's wife brought out a bottle of blackberry cordial she kept on hand for medicinal purposes.

After gulping half the contents, Elwin thanked the Moores and stumbled back to his horse.

Pete said to his wife, "Gladys will take care of him when he gets home. I have an idea he got his belly full of our romantic roundup the first day out."

Later in April, Fred came home from University of Arizona. He rode with his father every day during Easter vacation. The Moores, together with two cowboys, worked the whole east end of their range, putting what cattle they gathered into fenced pastureland. Pete grew more pleased with the calf crop tally every time he added numbers to his little black book.

The day before Fred returned to studies in Tucson, he and his father crossed the river and met Elwin and Ben near the Old Johnson Place. (In private, Pete refused to acknowledge Luscombs' new name for the ranch, The Wickiup.)

"How is your roundup coming, Elwin?"

"Excellent progress," the Easterner replied.

Ben motioned with his head. "You guys acomin' with us?"

"Sure," agreed Pete and Fred together.

Soon the foursome neared the cholla flats, acres and acres of "jumping cactus" growing close together, some taller than a man's head.

Elwin pulled up his horse. "I say, I'm not riding in there."

"We are," said Pete.

"I usually ride around these cholla patches."

"Suit yourself. We're riding through."

Ben added, "We're not exactly hunting a comfortable spot for a picnic."

Elwin looked at the narrow trail entering the close growth of sharp-spined cactus.

Fred rode ahead, followed by Ben, with Pete close behind.

Looking over his shoulder, Pete saw Elwin, head rigid, eyes staring, rein his mount and bring up the rear.

The men followed the narrow cattle trail that wound through the middle of the flats.

"There's Ol' Split Ear," called Ben, "on up the trail."

From the rear came Elwin's excited voice, "Shall we drive him?"

"Ain't no need," shouted Ben. "My bull...."

His advice was drowned out by Elwin's cry for help.

Pete turned his head in time to see Elwin's mount rear. Nose full of cactus spines, the blood bay backed into four cacti, filling his rump and tail with clumps of needle-covered cholla.

Elwin pulled the reins. His horse leaped into the air, came down, hit the ground and bucked up the trail. Still hanging to his mount's side, he started slipping...slipping off on the left. Straightening, he pulled back into the saddle. His mount pitched sideways. Elwin started sliding off on the right. Straining at the saddle horn, he squirmed into the saddle again.

"Ride 'em cowboy!" yelled Buzzard Ben, easing ahead on the narrow trail.

Fred and Pete urged their mounts forward with due care.

The blood bay shook his head, pawed at his nose and kicked his rear end high in the air. Elwin flew out of the saddle. He grabbed the horse around the neck with the grip of a drowning man clutching a floating log. The horse came down on all fours, plopping the rider back into his seat, and stood trembling.

Pete grabbed the reins and held the horse's head. "Easy, boy. Easy."

Ben stopped laughing long enough to blow his nose on the ground. "Great smolderin' piles of cow crap. Ain't nobody, but nobody can ride a horse that good." He glanced at Elwin, who was trembling worse than the horse under him. "What kept you on?"

The dude's voice was tremulous. "It was like riding into the valley of the six hundred—cactus to the left of me, cactus to the right of me." He slid off his horse and stood, holding the left stirrup for support. "If it is all right with you gentlemen, I believe I shall return to my headquarters. When reaction to the shock sets in, I know I shall need a strong drink."

The blood bay had turned around on the trail, and by dragging his nose on the ground had knocked off the clumps of cactus. Pete dismounted and worked gingerly with his knife and tobacco-stained fingers to pull out some of the last needles.

"Hold him up, Dad," Fred called. Easing close, he kicked the worst of the chollas loose from the horse's rump.

Elwin, taking the reins in his right hand, took two experimental steps toward home.

"Ain'tcha goin' to get on your horse?" asked Ben.

"Not until I am safely out of this hellish place."

"Don't make any fast moves," cautioned Pete.

"I am not going to make any moves," said Elwin, stepping very carefully ahead of his horse. "I am going to hold my breath and inch my way to open ground. Good day, gentlemen."

The three cowmen rode single file through the cholla flats toward the hills. In the lead, Fred mused, "Imagine a man walking when he can ride."

"Or hangin' on to a buckin' horse like a prize-winnin' rodeo rider," Ben added.

"When you talking about a dude," Pete said, "you can't stretch your imagination to cover what he might do. By the way, how is he getting along with his gathering?"

Buzzard Ben laughed shortly. "Them two drugstore cowboys of his would rather ride the road to town than ride the range. However, he's got most of them big steers in."

"And his yearlings?"

"It'll surprise me if he gathers half of 'em."

Pete twisted around in the saddle. "Can't you see that dude when the cattle buyers come around contracting early next spring? I can hear Elwin talking, 'I say, a certain percent of my yearlings this year will be two-year-olds.'"

Ben chuckled. "Then next year it'll be, 'If I can manage to corral them, a certain percent of my yearlings this year will be mixed two's and three's.'"

"You sound more like him than I do," Pete admitted. He stopped grinning and looked seriously over his shoulder. "You don't suppose we'll have to put up with the damn knucklehead forever, do you?"

Ben shrugged. "You said a dude ain't figureable." He spurred his horse. "Hurry up. Fred's gettin' ahead."

Pete urged his mount up the trail. *When is that Easterner going to quit playing cowboy, sell out and leave?*

Birth And Burros

The most difficult part of spring ranch work was over so far as Pete was concerned. He had seventy-five percent of his calves branded, tallied and turned back on the range. Roundup was near end. Gathered yearlings were in the fields at headquarters.

On May first Pete and his cowboys began hunting the last cattle along the river. He didn't send word to his dude neighbor to come over. As he explained to one of his men, "When Elwin's home, at least he's home. When he's riding, he's liable to be anywhere, and most generally in the wrong place."

That evening Pete returned home to find a note from his wife.

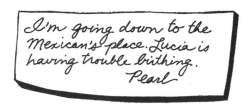

I'm going down to the Mexican's place. Lucia is having trouble birthing.
Pearl

Pete slid his arms out of the warm sleeves of his denim jacket. Then he fired up the wood stove, put on a pot of coffee, and sat down to wait. It wasn't long before Pearl came in the back door followed by the Luscombs and Buzzard Ben.

Ben sailed his hat across the kitchen and squatted down next to the stove. "That Mexican woman hasn't missed spring. She calves every year, same as a cow."

Pete scowled and motioned with his eyebrows to Gladys.

Ben caught the message he was supposed to watch his strong language in the presence of ladies and laughed. "After what we've been through this afternoon, we're all used to plain talk."

The Eastern woman spread her hands to the warmth of the fire. "Honestly, I had no idea what I was getting into."

"Nor I," agreed her husband.

Pearl washed her hands at the sink and began preparing the evening meal. "Make yourselves at home. I'll soon have supper ready."

"Let me help," Gladys offered, stepping up to the sink.

Pete squatted on the floor with his back against the wall. "Is all this palaver about Lucia having a baby? It's never been news before."

Mixing flour and lard in a large blue enamelware bowl, Pearl answered, "Early in the afternoon, Maria—she's the oldest—came here and said her mama needed help. When I asked about her father she said he took the rest of the kids with him to get the doctor in town."

"All those kids?" Pete asked.

"No, only the four youngest. The others are visiting his sister. Anyway, when *her* sister hadn't come to help, Juan got worried."

Gladys said, "Elwin and I were there to trade for some little green onions, weren't we dear?"

Elwin took his palms from under his chin and answered his wife. "I say, we never did get them."

"Then Ben came."

Pete looked at his neighbor with a look that asked, "What were you doing, tracking the dude's wife?"

Gladys pressed her palms together. "I can still see that poor woman chewing on an old towel."

"Who delivered the baby?" Pete asked.

"Ben," said Gladys.

"Gladys," said Ben at the same time.

Pearl smiled and added water to the mixing bowl.

Elwin dropped his chin into his cupped hands. "I went to double check. Found the doctor and Juan with his children driving toward the house."

"By the time you showed up, the show was over," Ben said with a chuckle.

"It was a breach," Pearl explained and Maria had hard labor, but she finally gave birth to another healthy baby, a girl.

Pete rubbed his shoulders against the wall and got to his feet. "I'll be back." He breathed deeply of the beef and chili simmering on the stove.

At the corral he leaned against his horse and rolled a cigarette. He felt the loose flakes of tobacco spill in his hands, as he rolled the paper in his fingers. Away from the house in the late spring evening, there were no distracting sounds—only the wonderful kind of quiet that to him was sweet music humming in his ears.

Ben left the house and joined him. "Need any help?"

Pete held lighted match to the end of his "roll-your-own".

Without answering, he inhaled deeply and continued his thoughts.

Speaking aloud, he said, "That woman had twelve kids, no trouble at all. Then with number thirteen she has complications. Me? I live happy on a cattle ranch till I'm sixty years old. I'm free. I have no troubles I can't handle myself. All of a sudden my life is full of complications—dudes."

Ben laughed. "You're hungry."

"And you're always bragging about something. Still and all, I didn't know you included midwifing."

"Hell, I don't, but Gladys—"

"If Gladys asked you to squat and drop a little green ring around yourself, you'd do it."

"Ah, Pete, she was just as good as a Western woman tonight. Hey, did you notice she's cut off her long red fingernails?"

"You know better than to go into a Mexican woman's bedroom when she's...you know. Why, she'd rather die than—"

"I didn't. I stayed outside the door and explained about all the calves I've pulled. I gave lots of helpful advice on how to turn that baby around."

"Bull!"

"I did. 'Course I don't know how much of my help Gladys used, but between her an' Pearl they got the baby borned. Soon as I heard the baby bawl I went out to see if Elwin had maybe left the bar in his car unlocked."

"He hadn't."

"No, but he sure came out, got a bottle an' shared real neighborlike."

There was no more talk for several minutes, only sounds of breathing, scrape of the metal bit pulled from the horse's mouth, and rattle of the buckle as Pete carried his saddle into the barn.

Ben chuckled. "After it was all over, you woulda got

a kick outa Gladys."

"She fainted?"

"Naw. Worse'n that. She knows I talk Spanish, so she made me translate while she set out to give the new mama a lecture of what she called birth control."

The two men leaned against the corral fence. Pete felt himself begin to chuckle. "I can imagine you helping at the birthing better than I can figure you for telling that Mexican woman anything like that."

"Oh, I didn't tell her what Gladys said. I told her the angel with the red hair said it was the most beautiful baby in the world an' she hoped she'd have a million."

"Yeah, an' what did you tell Gladys?"

"I told her Maria was tickled to death to get such valuable information."

"She'll have another baby next spring."

"Sure, an' I didn't break my stick with the redhead."

Without warning the back screen door of the house opened and Gladys rushed out screaming. Pete and Ben ran toward her.

"Now what?" asked Pete between huffing and puffing as they entered the kitchen.

Elwin, his eyeballs straining at their sockets, sat at the table. He clutched at his throat and beat the floor with his boot heels.

"Is this an asthma attack?" Pete asked Pearl.

Shaking her head, she forced a spoon of lard at Elwin. "Swallow," she ordered.

Elwin gulped the spoon of grease. Tears streamed from his blinking eyes.

"Ohhhh, Elwin," cried Gladys, holding his head to her bosom.

"We were talking," explained Pearl. "He put a whole handful of chili peppers into his mouth and chewed on them before I could warn him."

"I thought they were like salted peanuts," said Elwin between gasps. He blew out his breath and stared as though he expected to see the rising heat waves.

Ben slapped his thigh. "Man, there's gonna be more'n your mouth an' throat on fire. Tomorrow your other end will fire up."

Pete reached into the bowl at the center of the table and picked out one of the round, wrinkled, pea-sized pods. Rubbing it between thumb and forefinger, he broke the brown skin and let the tomato-like seeds fall on the white oilcloth. "There's enough hot pepper here to season a whole pot of beans."

"Water," yelled Elwin. "Water!"

Pearl shook her head. "I told you that is the worst thing you can do. Here," she said, handing him a thin flour and water pancake from the top of the stove. "Chew this tortilla."

Pete walked over to the stove and stirred the contents of the pot. "What are we having, burros?"

"Burro?" asked Gladys. "Isn't a burro a small horse-like animal native to Arizona?" She looked around Pete's shoulder into the pot. "Isn't the meat top round of beef?"

Ben laughed. "It's liable to be anythin' from wild hog to jackrabbit, but jackass would be my guess."

Elwin, holding his throat with his left hand, joined the people at the stove and moved the spoon in the kettle. "Upon close scrutiny, I find it difficult to ascertain the origin of this particular meat now or prove—"

Ben interrupted, "Aw, who cares. Haven't you ever been hungry?"

"No," said the Easterner, putting his half-eaten tortilla on the table, "and I don't think I am now." He sat down.

Gladys sniffed the air above the kettle. "Surely nothing that smells so delicious could be cooked donkey."

Except for a mouthful of dried beef, Pete had eaten no food since his four o'clock breakfast. He watched Pearl pat a dough ball between her palms until it was the size of a dinner plate and then flip it onto the top of the wood stove. After a few seconds she reached out, grabbed an edge with bare fingers and turned it over.

Gladys tried to follow Pearl's movements. "Oh, dear, look what happened to mine." She had poked a hole in the middle of the tortilla. The uncooked flour and water pancake was sagging in her hands like a wet paper towel.

Pete leaned against the sink. "Let's don't bother about sitting down for supper. I'd like to eat standing right here."

Gladys, gathering up the ends of the sagging tortilla in her hands looked at Pete, her eyes wide. "Why, Mr. Moore, I didn't think a man who lives on a horse the way you do would ever eat standing up."

"I don't usually, but I'm hungry. I figure I'll get faster service from stove to hand to mouth without detouring by the table."

Elwin flipped his half-eaten tortilla absently against the oilcloth, held his mouth open, and panted like a tired dog.

Pearl flipped another cooked tortilla onto one of the plates on the drainboard. She put a heaping tablespoon of hot, chili-spiced shredded beef off circle's center and began rolling. After turning under the end of the roll, she handed the burro to Pete. "Show them how we eat it."

Her husband held the roll first in one hand and then the other, treating it like a hot potato. He blew breath over the open end to cool it before he took a quick bite.

Pearl kept busy between stove and drainboard.

Gladys pinched off another wad of the raw dough. "There must be an easier way to flatten these balls. I need a floured board and a rolling pin."

"I need food," said Buzzard Ben.

"A burro for you," said Pearl, "and for you, Mr. Luscomb."

Elwin shook his head. "No more heat, thank you. Is this a Mexican dish or Indian? Such hot chili must be unadulterated wild Indian."

Pete saw Gladys nudge her husband. Elwin failed to understand his wife's signal, which Pete translated as meaning, "Please, dear, don't make belittling remarks about Indians in front of Pearl. She's part Apache."

In the silence Elwin glanced at Pearl, standing immobile, a stove lid in one hand and a piece of mesquite wood in the other. The moment passed and he continued his line of thinking. "I wish I were part Indian. I sometimes feel the white man could do with more hardiness." Warming to his subject, the Easterner stared at the ceiling. "How I'd like to be able to go for days on foot, over rough terrain, for fifty miles."

"You'd have to dig around a lot," Ben said, teetering in his chair, "to find an Injun that good." He stepped to the back door, opened the screen, and spat outside.

Pete walked past him to get an armload of firewood.

Elwin's voice rose. "Every overturned stone, every broken twig and branch would tell me what is going on."

Ben followed Pete and whispered, "It'll take more'n a broken twig for that dude to know what's goin' on."

"He tries and he's an all-right guy, but will he ever

129

really understand cow business?" Pete asked, stacking mesquite knots on his arm. "I hope they leave before long. I'm too tired to talk anymore tonight."

The Luscombs cooperated with Pete's hopes and went home half an hour later.

Around midnight, Pearl shook her husband's shoulder. "Roll over...snoring and muttering...you must be dreaming."

Pete blinked and sat up. "You're right. I was playing stud poker at the pool hall in town. Elwin was the big winner. He kept raking in the chips—cow chips."

Woolly Wonders

On the last day of his river riding, Pete met one of his neighbors on horseback. "Hi, Ben," he called reining alongside. "If you see the Eastern dude anywhere around in the next day or two, tell him I've gathered his stuff out of the brush, will you?"

Ben didn't return the greeting with his usual grin. Instead he rode his horse close and said, "Elwin don't care 'bout a few head of cattle you might have of his. He's off on a new project." Ben removed his wide-brimmed hat and ran his fingers through a thatch of unruly hair. "Get ready for a shock, and I don't think you'll believe it till you see it with your own eyes."

"Quit 'coyoteing' around the edge. You know nothing those Eastern visitors do can surprise me any more."

"Dammit, they bought the Old Johnson Place. They're not visitors."

"They'll always be visitors."

"All right, you stubborn ol' jackass, but what they bought will surprise you."

"Then spill it. You know I'm not going over to their damned Wickiup to look at one more thing."

Ben reined to a stop and leaned over the pommel of his saddle. "You wouldn't bet that horse you're ridin' against a couple hundred dollars, wouldja?"

"No," answered Pete, riding on.

Ben raised his voice. "Well, Elwin ain't holdin' his yearlin's until May. Trucks come in yesterday an' took what he had to Tucson."

Pete stopped his horse and snorted. "He's losing ten dollars a head on them by selling so soon. Nothing new. He's lost more money than that on lots of his moves." He scowled. "What's it to you?"

"I'll tell you what. Elwin has gone an' bought him a herd of runny-nosed sheep."

"*Sheep!*" Pete screamed the word. "He can't do that."

"Maybe he can't, but his wife says he did...all right. I seen 'em."

The two men loped their horses toward the river crossing and hit the road to the Old Johnson Place. They galloped straight to the sixty acres of irrigated green feed growing in a strip along the river east of the corrals. A band of white woolly animals ran in a bunch to the far end of the long field.

Pete stopped his mount and stared with disbelief. "There must be a hundred head. Is Elwin quitting the cow business?"

Ben shook his head. "Gladys says it's just a sideline."

"Then by God, they'd better keep their sideline damn well penned up."

"Don't pop off at me. I'm with you. Are you goin' to threaten Elwin?"

"No, but I'll tell him he hasn't a fence that will hold these snot-nosed woolly bastards, and I'll be within my legal rights if I take a potshot at every one that shows up on my land."

They rode toward the house at Luscombs' headquarters and saw Elwin standing in his yard. He strode to the fence, arm upraised in greeting, a welcome smile on his face.

Pete said, "I see you're in the sheep business."

"Not to any great extent. I simply want some animals to clean my ditches and utilize my feed."

"You'd better keep them home, or you won't have so many to do the utilizing," Pete snapped.

Elwin's smile grew broader. "When I made that same remark to you, Ben, and asked you to keep your split-eared bull at home, you informed me I could fence the brute out if I didn't want him on my place." He stepped back two paces. "I say, if you gentlemen do not want sheep on your ranches, fence them off."

Pete urged his horse forward a step. "Mr. Luscomb, there is a herd law on sheep."

Elwin pursed his lips, looked at the ground, and drew a circle on the greening lawn with his polished boot tip. Raising his head slowly, he said, "Hummm. I'm a lawyer, but not familiar with...herd law, you say?"

Ben spoke up. "It means you have to have a sheepherder."

"Or fence them in," added Pete, clenching his false teeth.

The Easterner straightened his shoulders and took a deep breath. "If this is true, I shall construct a good fence at the earliest possible moment."

Pete said, "It takes netting wire to hold them."

Elwin nodded, staring back at the ground.

Satisfied, the men started to ride away, when Pete noticed the newly landscaped yard. He pointed to wide-leafed plants along the west fence. "That's castor bean." He looked along the east hedge. "And that's oleander."

"Yeah," Ben agreed, "an' go look in the flower boxes."

The men dismounted, tied their horses, and entered the yard. Elwin led the way toward the house. All were careful to keep their feet on the flagstones.

Gladys came out the front door smiling. "My, it's been a long time since you've come over to our Wickiup, Mr. Moore."

"Yes, ma'am." After one quick look at the plants in the flower box, Pete asked, "Did you actually plant larkspur on purpose?"

"Of course," she said, stepping to her plants and touching the tops. "I raised them from seed. I had remarkable good luck. I understand that is to be expected with native growths."

Pete felt his neck swelling with anger. He swept the Luscombs a scathing glance. "Don't you know that stuff poisons cattle?"

"So does oleander an' castor beans," put in Ben.

Gladys clapped her hands and tossed her red hair. "Don't look so concerned. Cattle won't get in our fenced yard."

"What if some knothead leaves a gate open?" Ben asked.

"And the seeds," Pete added. "Seeds will blow all over the country, and we've almost got the range clear of this stuff."

Gladys held open the front door. "Surely you exaggerate. Cattle have other things to eat. Wait, won't you come in? Or would you rather go out to the corrals and see my dairy calves? I put the Flying G L brand on them myself."

"We can't stay," Pete answered, clenching his hands to help hold his temper. "Some other time?" He tipped

his hat and walked with Buzzard Ben to the gate.
Elwin stopped coiling a garden hose and waved.

"Good luck," called Ben, swinging into his saddle.

Pete mounted, and the two men rode toward the river crossing. Pete fumed, "It looks like Luscombs have to keep proving what damned fools they are."

June 17th Pete shipped his cattle to market. The yearly job was carried off with precision brought about by years of practice. Fred took leave from school to help. He, two cowboys, and three extra men gathered yearlings out of home pastures at dawn, drove them to corrals at headquarters, where they were sorted and weighed on stock scales. The crew then drove the herd ten miles to a siding outside a mining town. At high noon they loaded the animals onto cattle cars at the railroad stockyards to be shipped west to the Salt River Valley a hundred miles away.

Riding home horseback beside Fred that late June afternoon, Pete said, "Another year's work paid for and gone."

Dust swirled around their mounts' hooves. Knowing they were homeward bound to be unsaddled and fed, horses needed no urging.

Fred remarked, "Dad, I notice you're not as happy as you usually are on the windup of shipping day."

"You're right. In the past I could look ahead to a nice clean start with heavier calves next year and lots of rain."

"You still can."

"I'm too busy worrying about our Eastern neighbors. I can't tell where they're going to jump or whether I can get out of their way fast enough."

"Quick as you are, you'll manage."

Pete stared long and hard at his son. "When do you

suppose those dudes will get fed up playing cowboy and leave?"

"Ben said you asked him the same question the day Elwin almost got bucked off in the cholla patch. He didn't know the answer. I don't either. Dad, they may stay longer than we do."

Dance At The Moonshiners

Fourth of July was a day of celebration for the people along the lower San Pedro River. All yearlings had been shipped, ranch chores caught up, and the local folk felt it was time for relaxation.

The Moores' extended family—unmarried son, four daughters and spouses—began the day with a picnic under cottonwood trees at the lower pasture. Some went to town afterward to take part in a home-talent rodeo, but most finished off the day at a dance on the west side of the river. The affair was held in a barn near a schoolhouse which was abandoned when repeal of Prohibition forced moonshiners out of business. When they left, they took their children with them.

On the night of the Fourth, Pete, his wife and son, dressed in Sunday best outfits, drove in their Ford to the expected night of fun. They waited until nine o'clock for cooler weather.

Pete slid behind the wheel so that Fred could hold his banjo. Driving along in the hot evening, Pete said, "I've kept you too busy since you came from school this summer for you to work out much on that banjo. Figure you can keep up with the boys tonight?"

Pearl made an unlady-like snort. Smoothing the skirt of her square-dance dress, she said, "Fred's going to lead."

Pete slowed down, switched off the lights, and waited for a cow to cross the road. When he resumed driving, no one spoke.

Fred twanged the strings of his instrument during the rest of the short drive.

By the time the Moores arrived for the dance, people had already gathered. Parking the Ford on the west side of the schoolhouse, Pete sighed with relief. "There's cars from town, lots of horses and trucks. But look." He pointed to a big green sedan. "Except for the Luscombs' car, I don't see any sign of dudes."

At the opened doors of the barn, the Moores were greeted with shouts of welcome. "Hook-'em-cow!" yelled Buzzard Ben, clapping Pete on the shoulder. "I ain't seen hide nor hair of you since shippin' day. Good evenin', Pearl...hey, where you goin' Fred?"

The young man was half-way across the room when Pete felt another hand on his shoulder. It was Elwin. "I say," said the Easterner and his wife together, "it is good to see our neighbors."

Gladys stepped forward, admired Pearl's full-skirted dress, then smoothed flounces on her lavender-sprigged outfit. The two walked arm in arm toward the group of ladies sitting on benches near the orchestra.

Musicians were arranging themselves as best they

could on the makeshift platform.

Pete leaned against the wall at one side and watched his son move around, clapping hands, bending, bowing—trying to keep the artists happy, he decided.

"Hey, Gonzalez," Fred said, "don't you want to come closer to the front of the stage with that guitar?"

"But no," said the Mexican, almost dropping a leg of his chair off the platform, as he inched to get nearer his wife. Guitar slung around his neck, he placed his chair nearest the wall where Helen sat after she opened and set up his music stand.

"That's fine," Pete heard Fred say. "The accordion and bull fiddle in the back; guitar, mandolin, and banjo along here. We'll start with a fast schottische to get everybody in a good mood."

Pete hurried across the dance floor to his wife. "Did you notice as soon as Fred twanged on his banjo, the room filled with dancers faster than a pen full of dogied calves at feeding time?" He groaned. "This old concrete floor is hard on my feet."

Pearl, looking more Indian than usual in her red, pleated skirt, took her husband's arm. "Isn't this fun?" Hip to hip they began the one-two-three-kick steps.

The room was full. A dozen onlookers stood outside the opened doors of the old barn. In spite of the sultry July night, women wore full-skirted cotton dresses, and men wore Levi's, long-sleeved shirts, and boots. Music, if not the truest of key, was loud—heavy, throbbing beat accentuated by the foot tappings of musicians and dancers.

After two rounds of the floor, Pete stopped beside a bench near the orchestra. "I'm not as young as I used to be," he complained.

Pearl sat and inched close to Helen Gonzalez. Pete started toward the door, but Pearl grabbed her husband by the hip pocket. "Dance isn't over yet," she said.

Pete grinned and swung her onto the floor again. "These boots sure weren't meant for dancing," he protested, trying to wriggle toes as he kicked his foot forward on count four. They brushed another dancing couple.

"C'mon, you withered old prune," Buzzard Ben taunted. "Loosen up. You're movin' like a sore-footed ol' bull comin' down outa the rocks." He kicked without caution and swung his small partner to the opposite hip.

Pete turned Pearl in a tight circle as though reining his horse around a gopher hole and whispered, "That's Ben's California gal."

"He's courting two women tonight?" Pearl whispered in turn. "The widow from town he's been keeping company with is here, too."

"All I hope is they don't get together. I don't know much about that little California gal, but that tall widow-woman is wild, tough, and she—" Catching his wife's eye, Pete swallowed and stopped speaking abruptly. He also stopped dancing, and it was a mistake. Someone's foot from the circling crowd caught him behind the knees, and Pearl was barely able to hold him up.

Pete danced his wife outside onto the bare ground. "By grab, it's been a long day."

"I told you to wear your old boots. Take it easy if you want to. I'll visit with the girls, but when the square dancing starts, I expect to dance *Birdie In The Cage* with you." She joined a group of women by the corner of the building.

With a sigh of relief, Pete peered through the darkening, muggy night in search of male companions. He walked past two groups of talking, laughing people until he found a knot of men. Six cowboys formed a semicircle at the rear of Elwin Luscomb's big green sedan. A small light in the trunk of the parked car showed rows of gleaming bottles and glasses, together with mixes.

As Pete approached, he heard one of his sons-in-law remark, "I'm glad we invited the Easterner to our shindig. This is what I call real hospitality. Wow, Elwin sure buys good hooch."

Recognizing the voice, Pete recalled how often it was he had at least one of his daughters' husbands around under foot. He recognized another voice saying, "The thing I like about the dude's whisky is that it ain't scarce."

Pete stepped up. "Hi, Ben. How in the world did you get out here so fast? When I saw you last you were thrilling that little California woman with your crow-hopping."

The men guffawed. Ben smacked his lips and laughed. "When the first dance was over, that town widow-woman come chargin' me like an ol' cow on the fight, so I dodged an' ducked for cover."

From the barn at the side of the old schoolhouse came the fast tempo of a hoedown. Pete leaned against the car.

Ben clinked glass on bottle. "Get while the gettin's good, boys. Elwin usually keeps this stuff locked up."

Another man joined the group, saying, "Ben, it's good you're getting fortified. There's a woman hunting you."

Ben's gulp was loud. "Were her eyes cold and green or black and flashin'?"

"Blazing!"

Pete tapped Ben on the back. "He's talking about the widow woman."

141

"Yeah," agreed the long-nosed cowboy, "an' here comes the moon to help her spot me."

Music stopped and dancers poured out of the stuffy barn into the sultry July night. Fred, banjo in hand, shouted, "First square dance coming up. Room for two squares inside, any number outside. I'm calling *Birdie In The Cage.*"

Ben said, "Uh-oh. I promised my California gal I'd dance this with her."

Pete groaned. "I promised Pearl." Dragging his feet across the ground between the parked vehicles and tethered horses, he mumbled, "Looks like Fred could have put it off for awhile. I'll bet his mother told him to make this the first square dance of the evening."

In spite of his maneuvering, Pete found himself in the set with Ben and both his girl friends. Ben and "California" were couple one, Pete and Pearl couple two, Gladys and Elwin couple three. The town widow, paired with an odd man from the stag line, rounded out the square. Pete noticed both girl friends had elbowed their way into being near Buzzard Ben.

Up on the platform Fred leaned his banjo against his chair and stood to make the calls. After his one-two signal, the country-western players began a fast tune while Fred sang out, "First gent swing the right-hand lady with a right hand 'round, a left to your own as you come down."

Pete stood, easing his weight from one sore foot to the other.

Ben cut across the square, gave Pearl a twirl and returned to "California."

Music poured from the platform as all strings and accordion twanged together. Fred raised his voice and called, "Swing the opposite lady with a right hand 'round, a left to your own as you come down."

As gentleman number one, it was Ben's show for the first chorus. Pete watched him go across the square, swing Gladys and return to his partner.

Pete waited for Fred to call, "Swing the left-hand lady with a right-hand swing." The flashing-eyed widow from town was waiting for Ben. As he clasped her hand and made a fast turn, she stepped down hard on his left foot, pulled back on his right arm and let go. Ben reeled backward into the next set.

"Birdie in the cage and seven hands 'round," continued Fred from the platform. Ben hurried back to his place and circled clockwise around "California."

Under his breath, Pete joined his son in the next call, "The bird hops out, and the crow hops in; keep on going around again."

Inside the circling ring of dancers Ben looked like a trapped rabbit, as he ducked and darted looks from under his eyebrows. His gaze slid past Pearl, jumped from Gladys to "California" to meet the eyes of his town widow.

Pete chuckled. "He can't stay away from her. Only way he can get out of the ring is with a hand clasp with lady number four."

Ben kept dancing and followed Fred's call, "The crow hops out with a left allemande, a right to your partner with a right and left grand."

For the next few minutes Pete didn't do a lot of thinking. As gentleman number two he repeated steps Ben had finished. He managed in spite of aching feet.

While Elwin repeated the steps as third man, Pete watched Ben and almost laughed aloud. "Poor old buzzard," he whispered to his partner. "He's been trying to grab hold of Gladys Luscomb for a year. Now she's in his arms, but he's so busy watching out for two other women, he doesn't realize he's hugging the red-

143

head at last."

Pete heard the dance come to a close with Fred's last call, "It's a hand-over-hand around the ring, and a hand-over-hand that dear little thing. Now when you meet, just swing and swing."

Partners were still swinging when Pete stopped. "Pearl, don't you think that's enough?"

Giving her husband a stony stare, Pearl flipped her red skirt. "If I do much dancing tonight, I'm going to have to find another partner."

Mopping his brow, Pete strolled over toward the orchestra. Elwin grabbed his elbow and exclaimed, "Look, Gonzalez is a left-handed guitar player."

"He calls himself *mano surdo*. I feel sorry for him. He has to rope across the saddle."

"Why?"

"Because horses are usually trained to run to the left side of the animal. I'm going outside and find a place to sit down. Too bad a man can't do his square dancing horseback."

Still holding Pete's arm, Elwin asked, "How do you manage your program? Do you trade dances?"

"Hell no. Grab a gal and stomp."

"In that event," said Elwin, dropping Pete's arm and starting for Helen Gonzalez, "it's the beautiful young blond for me."

"Except her," rasped Pete, clutching the Easterner's arm. "Don't stick your neck out or you'll find Gonzalez is not only left-handed but strong-handed."

Elwin whirled away. "Why? Her husband is busy playing, and she's done nothing but sit."

"Yeah," admitted Pete, "and she will all evening."

"Doesn't make sense." Elwin stopped as his voice boomed in the sudden hush of the room. He and Pete were alone in the center of the floor.

Fred grinned at his father and started the music. Both men bolted for the door. They met Ben charging in. "Hi," said Pete. "You sure looked like a birdie in a cage during that dance. Song must have been named for you."

Glancing furtively around at the dancers, Ben answered, "Wish I had a good strong cage to climb in right this minute."

The three men walked outside. Pete managed to stay away from the dance floor until intermission. During this period of rest for the musicians, everybody took time out to visit. They milled around, sat in or lounged against automobiles.

Bathed by the moonlight Pete sat in his Ford alongside Ben. They were talking about drought conditions on the range. Neither paid any attention to the laughing and shouting of the celebrators until Pete heard the start of an argument in the car parked next to his Ford. He nudged Ben and the two sat listening.

A feminine voice from within the car said, "I repeat, would you mind taking your feet down?"

Ben dug Pete in the ribs. "That's 'California' for sure."

On the broad fender of the late model car sat a tall woman. For an answer she laughed and beat a tattoo on the car with her heels.

"California's voice came again, "I asked you nicely to please stop kicking my car."

A laugh but no answer except the sound of high heels scraping paint off metal.

"California" leaned her head out the window and said, "If you won't get off my car, I'm going to take you off."

"You and who else?" answered the widow from town.

In the Ford Ben hunched down out of sight. Pete

grabbed him by the collar. "Get up," he hissed. "Your womenfolk are about to come to blows."

The front door of the new automobile opened and out stepped "California". Reaching up she took hold of the tall woman's arm and pulled her from the fender.

The widow turned and lunged. "You bitch."

A few feet away, Ben pleaded, "Let me outa here."

"Are you going to break up the fight?"

"Hell no. The widow woman will beat little 'California' to a pulp an' then start in on me."

The two women were in a close, snarling clinch, each refusing to let go the other's long hair.

Hearing sounds of the scuffle, people hurried forward, curious as a bunch of colts.

Gladys, standing out of the way on the other side of the Ford, leaned across the hood and said to Pete, "I think this is disgusting and no way for ladies to behave." Seeing Ben cowering, she added, "Aren't you going to stop the vulgar display?"

"No ma'am," he said, watching the tussle.

Pete, himself unhappy about the fight and uncomfortable being part of the situation, whispered to Ben, "If Gladys Luscomb doesn't like our morals or our manners, maybe she'll go back East."

There was nothing refined about the female scrap in progress. Flat on her back, the town widow was reduced to more name-calling, as "California" sat on her chest and slapped.

Ben gulped. "The little one's got more fight in her than I thought."

No one made a move to separate the women. Fred put an end to their scuffle when he called from the barn door, "We've had enough intermission. Music is about to start. Let's step."

Cold green eyes met blazing black ones, as the two

disheveled females scrambled to their feet. The widow hurried toward the outhouse; "California" sped off in her car.

A voice from the crowd gave a "Ya-hoo", adding, "Let's dance. Come on everybody, round 'em up and head 'em out."

Gladys said, "Are all your parties so uninhibited?"

"Las' Fourth of July we had knifin'," Ben said, "but this is the first—"

Pete cut him short. "Hear the horses whinny? They are riled up, too."

Ben cocked his head. "Listen. They're playin' *Put Your Little Foot.*"

"*The Varsouvienne,*" agreed Gladys, "my favorite Western dance."

"What are we waitin' for?" asked Ben, climbing out of the Ford.

"I'd better find Pearl before I get mixed up in a fight of my own," Pete said.

He found his wife and joined the dancing. The tempo of the music speeded up after intermission. Most of the dancers had imbibed freely and were singing, "Put your little foot, put your little foot, put your little foot right there."

Pete sang with a slight change of words, "Put your sore ol' foot," repeated over and over.

The room was full of cigarette smoke, pulsing music, and sweating bodies.

Pete noticed Ben dancing with Gladys. He said to Pearl, "The rascal can sure dance." They watched Ben's intricate footwork.

The crowd began watching as well, stepping back to give more space.

Gladys threw back her head and moved her voluptuous body with abandon. Her dance with Ben became

147

an exhibition.

Standing near the wall by the orchestra, Pete nudged Pearl. She followed his look. Elwin was holding Gonzalez's young blond wife by the hand and urging her to her feet. She pulled back.

Above her on the platform Gonzalez never missed a beat on his guitar, but he weaved his head, neck stretched, like a rattlesnake coiled ready to strike.

Pete shoved his way through the crowd. Before he could stop him, Elwin led the young woman onto the floor and took her into his arms.

"Not fair for a beautiful thing like you to sit out all the dances," the Easterner said, speech slurred.

Gonzalez, guitar swinging loose around his neck, shouted "*Caramba,*" and brought his music stand down on Elwin's head. The dude staggered across the floor and fell to his knees.

Musicians stopped playing, and dancers switched attention from the exhibition dance to the newest and loudest attraction. Sheet music slid along the concrete.

"Oh, Elllllwin," Gladys cried. She raced to her husband, who was still on his knees.

Taking Helen by the arm and music stand by the neck, Gonzalez marched from the barn. His guitar bumped his chest every step, while his chord notations lay forgotten on the floor.

"Whadaya know," Ben said to Pete. "Two knockdown-drag-outs and it's only midnight." He turned to Gladys, who was helping groggy Elwin to his feet, and asked, "If it's vulgar when two women fight over a man, what is it when two men fight over a woman?"

Elwin rubbed his hand over the top of his head. "I only wanted to dance with the young lady."

The tall widow grabbed Ben by the shoulder. "We were not fighting over you, you no account two-timer."

148

Ben ducked and ran for the opened doors. Eyes blazing, teeth gnashing, the tall woman strode after him.

"Oh, boy," said Fred, slapping the strings of his banjo, "if this winds up in another fight, we'll break the record."

In spite of the music, most of the people left the dance floor and crowded outside.

By the time Pete and Pearl walked across the old school playground, Ben had shinnied halfway up the flagpole. A tall woman stood below brandishing a two-inch pipe with both hands.

Bystanders cheered and hollered.

"Pearl," said Pete, "let's go home. I like a dance to be like a horse, full of spirit but sensible. This hootenanny is out of hand."

"What about Fred? He's still playing."

"Somebody is sure to see he gets home."

Pete started the Ford and backed out to the road. Ben was almost at the top of the swaying pole and climbing.

"Wiry and strong, isn't he? Too bad he's not smart enough to stay out of trouble in the first place. Did you notice he had his arms around Gladys again, but he was so busy showing off his fancy dance steps, he forgot to enjoy holding her...." His voice trailed off when he realized his wife did not enjoy discussing Buzzard Ben's chasing after a married woman. She sat quietly, her face unreadable in the moonlight.

Swinging east, Pete shifted into high gear and turned on the headlights, pausing long enough for one quick look over his shoulder. He saw Ben lose his grip and slide down the pole toward the arms of his town widow.

Pete drove on. After a long, drawn-out sigh, he said, "We always had fun at the Moonshiner's Place before we had outsiders. Sure, we got wild once in a while, but not crazy like tonight." He grasped the wheel and pushed the accelerator. "Goes to show what happens when dudes buy a ranch and try to be cowboys. They're not. They never will be, and all they do is stir up trouble."

They drove in silence for another mile. Pearl, holding the dashboard with both hands, said, "Next month there will be one more dude."

Pete turned his head and slacked speed.

Pearl relaxed her hand hold. "Gladys told me her daughter will be here the middle of August."

Pete clenched his teeth.

Pearl bounced on the rough-riding seat. "She thinks their daughter Lita and our son Fred have a lot in common. Both are twenty and Gladys says they probably share interests."

"Not *my* son. He'll never have anything to do with an Eastern girl."

"What if she's as pretty as her mother?"

Pete groaned. "Please don't talk like that."

"All right....Oh, I had fun dancing tonight."

"Gosh darn it all," said Pete, remembering as always to avoid using profanity in the presence of ladies. "The night is ruined, and now you're telling me something I can't sleep off."

Turning into their yard, he drove toward the shed.

"Try not to worry. Everything will work out."

"You had your way about who the girls married. I wound up with four town-loving sons-in-law I can't stand. I'll not have Fred mixed up with a dude woman." The Ford lurched to a stop. "And that's final."

The Rescue

Hot summer dragged on. Day after day storm clouds gathered. After weeks of build-up, thunderstorms broke and rains came. Pete and Fred saddled up early morning, middle of August, and rode out to check damage made by a heavy deluge the night before.

Pete said to his son, "It looks like the flood is worse than the one last year."

"I know, Dad. For the past two years we've averaged only four inches of rain."

"And now it comes all at once."

Young Fred inhaled deeply of heavy, muggy air. "I guess Gladys and Elwin are marooned again over at The Wickiup."

"Serves the dudes right."

"Now Dad, you're not going to start blaming the weather on poor defenseless Easterners. You're mad because they beat you out of buying the Old Johnson Place and added insult to injury by renaming it The Wickiup."

"Why not? It sure seems like God Almighty is riled

about something, the way he's sending gully-washers smashing and charging out of the hills."

The two men left headquarters and rode toward the river.

"No damage at home," remarked Fred, "that a couple of weeks hard work won't uncover and clean up."

"Do you figure we can get the fences repaired and the irrigating ditches cleaned out before you go back to college?"

"Could be." Fred turned around in the saddle. "I wonder if the concrete curbing I put around the spring is still standing." It was slow riding over the soggy river bank. Horses' hooves made little sucking sounds as they pulled out of the ground.

Almost an hour later the men reached to the crossing. They had taken a detour to a water tank and windmill off to the north toward town. There they found the mill in good working order with several head of cattle drinking clear water from a cement trough.

When they did arrive at the crossing, Pete gasped. "The old San Pedro has cut herself a new channel along here."

A few minutes later, Pete looked west across the river. "Dammit, I'll bet our spring is under water again."

Fred nodded. "Concrete curbing is probably standing."

"I notice Luscombs didn't lose any more land, and what sheep I can see are settled. At least Elwin has been good about keeping them fenced off the range."

"What do you suppose is going on at Ben's place?"

"Don't worry about ol' Ben," came a loud voice. "I'm settin' horseback right here in the brush. My place is on high ground, an' except for mushy corrals I didn't get hurt none, but them poor dudes woulda been washed back east 'cept the river don't go that direction."

When Ben rode into sight, Fred looked him over carefully. "It's still a good-sized river, and your horse is dry. How do you already know what's going on at Luscombs?"

"Well, Freddie boy, I just oughta let you worry that mystery 'round in your college-trained head an' see if you can come up with the answer, but I won't. I'll tell you. I spent the night in your barn. Hell, I couldn't get home. Before you did chores, I saddled up and checked the river."

"Why didn't you come to the house?"

"Dammit, 'cause I was lickered up." He pointed above the old crossing. "Gladys was standin' over there. We yelled back an' forth across the river till she got back on her horse and rode toward home."

Pete snorted. "You talked over all that roaring water?"

Ben nodded. "When Gladys went to jumpin' around an' wavin' her tits an' pointin', I guessed what she was sayin'. Look. Here she comes now."

From across the river came a muffled "Yoo hoo". Gladys, astride her black horse, was on the opposite bank. She made several waving and pointing motions.

Fred laughed. "All right. You say you understand that kind of talk. What is she saying?"

Ben took off his hat and ran rope-calloused fingers through unkempt hair. "Damned if I can tell this time." Putting on his hat, he beamed. "But ain't she pretty bouncin' around that way?"

"Good God!" Pete's voice exploded. "She's going to swim that black across the river. She doesn't know how. Horse'll turn over sure as hell."

The three men rode close to the bank, yelling and making what Pete hoped were explanatory motions. It was no use.

153

"Whatever is the matter," Ben said, "must be worse than I thought from the wavin' earlier. She's hittin' swimmin' water."

"Don't bet on what a dude will do," said Fred. "Dad and I met her riding across the crossing when they bought the Old Johnson Place last year, and all she wanted was to tell us somebody already had the G L brand."

As he rode along the bank, Pete nodded, watching Gladys. "Dudes don't have to have a reason for pulling dumb stunts. It comes natural."

The redhead, halfway across the river, was obviously having trouble. The black horse turned.

"Drop the reins," yelled Fred.

Ben galloped downstream and urged his horse into the water. He began hollering instructions even before his mount began swimming.

Gladys and her horse were going in a circle.

Pete, watching closely, said to his son, "She's got the horse panicked and she's scared herself. "Here, stay put. Two horses out there threshing around is enough."

Fred reined alongside his father. "There's really no need for Ben to save her. All he needs to do is help the horse to shore."

"Not Ben. Watch him come in with the redhead across his saddle."

"You called it, Dad. He's dragging her off the black. She looks like a soggy, rag doll...doesn't need to get her that wet. Does he think he is starring in a Grade B movie? Wait. I'll get her horse."

A few minutes later Fred, holding the reins of Gladys's mount, rode to meet Pete, who was helping Ben make a landing with the thoroughly wet and frightened woman.

"You saved my life," she gasped, taking in the three

men with one sweeping glance.

Ben bristled. "Now wait a minute. They didn't get out there an' have water swishin' up under their rear ends. I'm soaked. I'll have to take my saddle clear apart this afternoon, oil it, and dry the sheepskin."

"Sheepskin!" wailed Gladys. "Twenty-five of our sheep went down the river in the middle of the night. Muddy water is six inches deep in the houses, big rocks all over the yard, and I'm supposed to meet Lita in Tucson this afternoon."

"Lita?" repeated Fred, raising his eyebrows.

Looking at his son's obvious interest, Pete felt sweat pop out on his wrinkled forehead.

With disgust, Ben ran his hand under his saddle fenders and flipped water from his fingertips, while he mumbled to himself.

Gladys threw her arms around her horse's neck and leaned heavily. "Elwin went in the car early this morning, but I heard the weather reports and storm damage over the radio. Oh, I know he's stuck somewhere in a wash or had an accident." She shuddered, lifted her head and looked at Pete. "I was coming over to see if I could borrow your Ford and go to town and send a message."

"If your daughter is waiting in Tucson," Fred said, "you and I can make the trip in the Ford and bring her here."

Pete felt himself swelling like a cornered horned toad.

"Oh, no," Gladys said, mounting. "I couldn't possibly let you do that. I just couldn't...when can we start?"

"Right away," Fred answered. "As soon as we get to our place horseback, Mother will give you some dry clothes, and we'll be off."

"Thanks for the compliment, but your mother is

much smaller than I. Don't worry. I'll dry out on the trip."

Apparently hurt by being left out of the plans, Ben turned his horse toward the crossing.

Gladys waved and called, "Thank you, Ben. I won't forget your help. I promise I'll make it up to you one of these days."

Head down, Buzzard Ben spurred his mount into the river.

Pete turned toward home. Gladys followed and Fred brought up the rear, as the three proceeded single file along the road.

The men said very little, but Gladys, her brush with danger apparently forgotten, kept up a happy chatter. The only thing she said of any importance or interest to Pete was that her daughter was planning to stay ten days.

After Fred gassed the Ford, he and Gladys left for Tucson.

Pete felt as helpless as a hobbled horse. He stood on the front porch, rolling and smoking cigarette after cigarette.

Hours later Pearl joined him, saying, "You've got the fidgets."

Peering into the dusk toward town, Pete said, "Fred ought to be back from Tucson with that pair of women."

Pearl's rocker inched across the wooden floor. "Don't worry about our son. He's our little boy, but—"

"Looks like one with that silly cut-off hair."

"But he's a man and you can't tell him every move to make."

"I won't tell him. I'll warn him."

At midnight Pete was sitting on the front porch asleep when the Ford's headlights cut across the yard and woke him. Dropping his boots from the ledge, he strode into the blackness of night to meet the travelers.

"Hi, Dad," called Fred, cutting the engine. "Don't tell me you've been waiting up for us. I hope Mother has coffee left."

Gladys introduced her daughter, saying it was the first time she had done so in the dark.

"How do you do, Mr. Moore," came the young voice.

Pete felt her soft hand and mumbled greetings while the foursome stumbled across the rocky yard toward the house.

Pearl was already in the kitchen. "I saw the headlights coming. Coffee is ready, and Lita, you look the way I imagined."

How do you know? Pete thought. *She's taller and darker and lighter-boned than Gladys. Takes after her father except her front teeth don't have a gap, and as far as I'm concerned, she'd look a damn sight prettier if she was somewhere else.* A quick slurp of coffee burned the inside of his mouth. He swallowed the mouthful along with a whole string of curses. Everybody laughed, and the tension of the meeting was over.

Lita said to Pete, "I feel as though I know you. Mother and Daddy have written me so much about you and what helpful neighbors you and your family have been."

Pete choked. He made a studied effort of drinking coffee, watching Fred to see what his son thought of this Eastern girl.

When he couldn't tell, he tried to let his mind go blank.

"Honestly, Mr. Moore," said Gladys, attempting to draw Pete into the conversation. "Since leaving you, we've had one wild adventure after another."

157

"Tell about Elwin," prompted Fred.

"You won't believe this," said Gladys.

"Try him," Pearl suggested.

"Well, Elwin was about halfway to Tucson when he drove the car into a small—what do you call it, a gulch?"

"How big was it? Might have been a gully," Pete answered.

"Anyway," Gladys continued, "a wall of water came down out of the hills."

"And smacked him broadside," Fred added.

"Daddy jumped clear," said Lita.

"But the car rolled over and over downstream," put in Gladys.

Pete looked from one face to another. "Who is telling this story?"

"We're so relieved now it's over," said Gladys, "we all want to tell it. Poor Elwin walked about five miles before he found a truck willing to pick him up and drive him to Tucson, and do you know what that husband of mine did?"

Pete stared into his second cup of coffee. "No telling."

"He walked right into a display room in Tucson and bought a convertible off the floor...of course, with no trade-in."

Fred laughed. "Remember the saloon he had in the back of that green job? Can't you see all those glasses and bottles floating downstream?"

"Where is Elwin now?" Pete asked without joining the chuckles.

Lita leaned across the oilcloth-covered table. "He'll drive home tomorrow after the water recedes." Her smile to Fred was coy. "Daddy couldn't drive the new convertible over some of the rough spots we came over tonight, could he?"

Fred grinned. Brown eyes met blue.

Pete didn't try to read his son's mind. He was too busy with his own thoughts about Elwin and his adventure: *That dude, marooned on the wrong side of the river, his worthless cowboys off in his pickup, and he buys a convertible he can't get home in—about as smart as the dumb SOB usually shows to be.* Pushing back his chair and stretching, he said, "There's not much left of this night, and tomorrow means clean-up work."

"Yes," said Gladys, rising quickly, "we mustn't keep you any longer, and we have work to do tomorrow, too."

Gladys and Lita moved toward the door, with Pete almost shoving from behind. Then Gladys clapped her hands over her mouth and gasped. "We can't get home."

Pearl wiped her hands on her apron and said practically, "I know. I'll make up an extra bed on the porch. Come."

Pete looked helplessly at Fred, who only grinned.

Stalking toward the bedroom, Pete said to his son, "I thought it was bad enough when I got trapped behind the river and was forced to stay overnight at their house. Now they're at my house. Don't leave yet. Help me take off these muddy boots."

Sitting on the edge of the bed, he motioned to his right leg and waited for Fred to back up and bend over. Bracing himself, he stuck the boot between Fred's spread legs.

As Fred pulled up on the heel, he chided his father. "You were so busy worrying about Elwin, you forgot about Gladys and Lita not being able to get home." A boot thudded to the floor, and Fred reached for the other one.

Pete wriggled his toes. "I'll get those two dude

159

women home in the morning, if I have to throw them across the river."

"Now, Dad, you know you won't feel like that tomorrow. See you at breakfast."

Pearl entered the room as Fred left. Before she could say a word, Pete asked, "Do you think nature lets young men stay safe around pretty girls?"

"Were you?"

The only answer was a tomcat's caterwauling outside.

Flooded

Without disturbing his wife, Pete slid out of bed before dawn, built a fire in the wood stove and put a pot of coffee on to boil. Because he felt uncomfortable with an Eastern woman and her daughter sleeping on the front porch, he hurried with breakfast and slipped out the back door. He hoped Elwin Luscomb would drive back from Tucson, load up his women and take them back across the river. His Western hospitality had been stretched to the limit.

At a shop near the barn he collected hammer, sack of staples and puller. Fred had told him he would help repair fences this morning.

Staying away from the house, Pete worked around the pasture long past mid-morning, re-tacking barbed wire, splicing where necessary.

Nearing the corrals, he saw his son building loop after loop in a lariat for the young Eastern girl. Fred showed no interest in repairing fence. He had rigged up a saw horse with attached horns and was showing Lita how to rope.

Near noon Pete saw Lita go to the house. Even from a hundred yards away, he noticed how she swayed her slender hips and tossed shiny black hair away from her face.

Gathering up his tools, he hurried to meet his son, who was recoiling ropes. "If you've finished your visiting, I sure could use some help. Two cowboys are working ditch, and one man on a fence can't do much when all four wires are down."

"I'll be with you after lunch. Lita thinks ranch life is kicks. You know, she's never been on a ranch?"

"She should have left it that way." He took his son by the arm. "You have to watch Eastern girls. They don't operate like we do. Do they?"

Fred laughed and pulled away. "A girl is a girl."

"Yeah, and a filly is a filly, but some you can handle and some you can't." Pete turned on his boot heel and strode toward the barn.

After lunch Elwin, driving his new convertible from Tucson, arrived at Moores' headquarters. The new car was mud-splattered and white sidewalled tires were caked, but Elwin sat behind the wheel with the air of a charioteer. Flashing his gap-toothed grin, he leaped from the automobile and embraced Gladys and Lita. "A rising river will not be a problem to us for very much longer," he bragged.

"Why?" asked his wife and daughter at the same time.

Waving his arms expansively, Elwin explained, "I've already started on a new project."

Pete and Fred strode up in time to hear the conversation. Apparently both storm and new car were ancient history.

"Yes, indeed," continued the Easterner, continuing his enthusiastic description, "the workmen are at this minute on their way to build the piers on both sides of the river. You know, our old crossing has been changed somewhat by the flood water, but outcropping of granite now exposed will provide excellent foundations for the piers."

"Daddy, you're not making sense," said Lita. "What are you building?"

"Transportation across the river. We're going to have a suspended cable with a swinging car to pull across. We'll leave a car in a garage on this side, so that when the water rises we will not be forced to stay at home if we desire to go elsewhere. A magnificent idea, don't you agree?"

The women nodded.

"It sounds feasible," said Fred, "but expensive."

"Forget the expense," said Elwin. "Think of the convenience."

Pete turned, trudged across the yard and entered his house.

"Pearl," he said, "the Luscombs are at it again. They are about to add another couple thousand dollars to the price of the Old Johnson Place with no chance for return on investment."

Before he could explain, he heard Elwin calling from the back door. "I say, I want to ask a favor."

Pete groaned.

"I'm sure you have extra mounts. What do you say we saddle up and ride across the river to my place?"

"Thanks, but Fred and I have so much cleaning up to do here, we'll be weeks catching up. But you're welcome to a couple of horses if you're anxious to get along. Gladys's black is in the corral."

Elwin snapped his fingers. "Corral. That reminds me. I put one of your bulls in my corral before the storm. I do hope he's safe."

"You what!"

"I suppose we should feed him or let him out."

"What in hell did you corral him for?"

"It really was for the safety of my pure-bred bulls. They couldn't get back into the pasture as long as your bull...."

Pete didn't hear the end of the sentence. In a rush to saddle up and go see for himself, he hurried to the barn.

The others followed. For the next half hour there was a hurry to wrangle horses, sort through hair pads and blankets, and delegate saddles. Annoyed and disgruntled, Pete tuned out most of the conversation. He did hear Luscombs' daughter say that although she was unaccustomed to Western-style riding, she was familiar with an English saddle and loved horses.

Pete wanted to hurry on and check the bull by himself, but he forced himself to wait for Fred, Elwin, Gladys and Lita.

Mounted, they proceeded up the road, and forded the river at Moores' crossing. Pete led the way to the Old Johnson Place in tight-lipped silence. As he passed under The Wickiup sign with "Elwin and Gladys Luscomb" spelled in rope letters, he whispered to Fred, "When there's a dude around, you don't need a damned sign to know it."

The old cowman rode directly to the corral and checked his bull. "How are you, boy? Trying to starve you, are they? Come on, the gate is open, and if you want to give those sissy bulls a good whipping on your way out, you got my blessing."

The bull, sides gaunt, eyes hollow, trotted through the gate straight for the oncoming riders. The women screamed, Elwin yelped, and the three turned quickly and galloped off.

Fred reined around and helped his father drive the bull toward the south hills.

"You didn't have to turn him right at us, Dad."

Pete stroked his chin. "If I hadn't thought the bull was too hungry to fight, I'm damned if I wouldn't have sicked him onto that gap-toothed, brainless, no-good, sorry—"

"Take it easy," Fred interrupted. "Elwin doesn't know."

"Doesn't excuse him. If a man broke a law, that damned bookish lawyer would be the first to say not knowing was no excuse." Pete wheeled his horse around. "Let's gather up our outfits and get the hell out of here."

"Wait. Look."

Pete pulled his horse to a stop and saw Luscombs' house and yard for the first time since the storm. The lawn was rutted, shrubbery uprooted, and flowers washed away. A muddy watermark showed that six inches of water had poured through the house. The carport sagged, part of the west roof was gone, and the patio was a shambles.

"I hate to see property damaged," said Pete, "but like I always say, 'more good comes out of a storm than bad.'"

"Are you talking about the rain water filling dirt tanks and greening up the range?"

"No. I'm thinking of how the flood got rid of Gladys's castor beans, oleander and larkspur. The storm uprooted the cattle-poisoning weeds and sent them down the river before they had a chance to go to seed."

"Here comes our neighbors. Are you going to change the look on your face and keep your opinions to yourself?"

"Sure, I'll mind my manners, but you know what I

say."

"More good comes out of a storm than bad. I heard you."

In days following, Fred worked only afternoons with his father on their ranch. Bright and early every morning he saddled up, crossed the river and went to The Wickiup to help Luscombs and extra crew repair storm damage.

For the first three days, Pete protested the arrangement. After that, he said nothing. He waited impatiently for time when Fred would return to college courses.

In spite of Pete's lack of interest about the changes taking place at The Wickiup, Fred explained each morning's accomplishment in complete detail as he sat at home every day eating late lunch. Pearl seemed to enjoy hearing about the redecorating of Luscombs' house, but Pete suffered through mealtime talks.

The first day Fred came home he had little to say except how much mud there was to the square inch of floor space in the big house.

The second day he told of jacking up the crumbling adobe and laying new foundations on the west side under the carport and master bedroom.

The third, fourth, fifth and sixth days he spoke in detail of the work, saying all was going according to plan.

But on the seventh day Fred was late for lunch. Pete was breaking open a biscuit when his son, whistling *Buffalo Gals,* pulled up to the table. Pete glanced up, nodded, then jabbed his spoon into the sugar bowl. Pearl carried a platter full of tamales from the kitchen stove. The three sat eating for several minutes.

Pete sighed. Maybe the boy wasn't going to burden

166

them with dude talk. He hoped in vain.

"You know," said Fred, pointing a fork at his father, "Home Economics is Lita's major. She's artistic, too. Gladys is giving her free rein in the interior of the house."

The veins swelled in Pete's neck.

Pearl said, "Luscombs must not be putting the house back the way it was."

"I'll say not," agreed Fred, scraping corn shucks from another fat, mush-covered dab of chili meat. "Gladys sold all the bamboo stuff, the red curtains, and everything modern. She's going after the authentic Apache. She has a design running around the door frames." Fred stopped with a forkful of food mid-air and laughed. "I thought the darn thing was Greek-key configuration, but Gladys says it is an Apache word picture for 'meandering stream'. She read the symbolic designs right out of a book. Also, they're keeping theme consistent in using Indian spider web, butterfly, and star." After chewing a mouthful and swallowing, he continued, "I'm convinced the designs are primitive, but I still think the Apache snake looks like a handful of dice laid corner to corner."

Pete cleared his throat noisily. "Up to now you've been interested in growing feed, greasing tractors, and de-worming cattle. How long do we have to listen to this female talk about house decorating and Indian mumbo-jumbo?"

Pearl began, "Please...."

"It would please me if the dude women would paint the whole place the way it was—a nice turd mucky dun."

"But, Dad, I don't intend to turn interior decorator. I'm interested in any kind of progress." He turned to his mother. "Besides, Lita's pretty darned nice to listen to my plans. I told her about planting willow trees along under the river bank to protect against erosion, and she was plenty interested."

Pearl nodded.

Pete's fist pounding the table rattled dishes. "A dude woman is a dude woman. They're not interested in anything Western except the show and blow. Next thing you'll be telling me is how cute she looks standing on a box with a paint brush in her hand."

Fred pushed back his plate. "Now that you mention it, she *is* pretty—anywhere."

As he excused himself and left the table, Pearl put a hand on Pete's shoulder and smoothed his blue work shirt. "You don't need to worry until he starts telling her how pretty she looks bending over the kitchen stove."

Pete knocked over his chair, righted it, and followed Fred outside. "I oiled the tractor this morning and hitched up the 'V,' so if you're through eating we'll scoop out the ditch between the east and southeast fields."

"Sure," said Fred, barely opening his lips.

The two went out to the fields and worked till dark. That night they had nothing to say to each other.

For the next three days they had nothing to discuss except work at their own headquarters. The only thing Pete knew about what was happening at Luscombs' place was news their cable car crossing the river was finished and in operation. Pearl told him.

The second week of September Pete drove Fred to school. He gave him money to buy a secondhand car of his own and wished him well in his senior year.

Fred's thanks conveyed little warmth.

The men shook hands without making eye contact.

Pete tried to soften the parting. "See you Thanksgiving. Remember, son, I'm not trying to tell you how to run your life."

"Sure, Dad."

"Pick your friends to suit yourself."

"I will."

"Just don't try to ram them down my throat."

"Sure."

A Pastoral Scene

For the next two months Pete settled into his usual
ranch routine. He worked with Buzzard Ben doctoring
cattle, rode the high plateau with Gonzalez, and built
an overflow system on his home windmill. He made
a special point of staying away from the Old Johnson
Place. If the Easterners wanted to buy a ranch next
to his, dude it up, rename it "The Wickiup, Elwin and
Gladys Luscomb," it was no longer any concern of his.

Early in November, after the first killing frost sent
yellowed cottonwood tree leaves floating to the
ground, he found one of Elwin's calves, showing signs
of having eaten poison weed. Its hindquarters were
unsteady, as Pete drove it to The Wickiup.

After corraling the calf, Pete reined his horse
around and looked for either of the Luscombs. He
hoped to find either husband or wife outside, because he had no desire to go to the house, be invited
in and forced to visit.

Seeing Elwin horseback out by the gate, he rode up
to deliver his message. Staring fixedly at his right boot

tip, he called out, "One of your calves got her belly full of goldenrod, so I put her in your corral. She'll probably be all right if you get her on green feed."

When his neighbor didn't answer, Pete looked up to see him rein his horse carefully and answer as carefully, "Thank you." He slowly raised a sharp-pointed pole, fully fifteen feet long.

Pete stared. "What's that thing?"

"An Apache lance. Authentic, too."

"What do you plan on doing with it?"

"I am attempting to satisfy my curiosity. I have bows and arrows, but I understand the Apache warrior carried this lethal weapon into battle, riding at full gallop, holding it aloft."

Elwin knotted his reins, dropped them on his mount's neck, and took the fifteen foot lance in both hands. "I'm of the opinion it can't be done."

"A gun would be simpler."

"But completely lacking in romantic appeal. Now the theory, as I understand it, is that one rides by controlling the horse with knee pressure. However, I shall attempt first to test balance."

"Wait," called Pete, as Elwin gouged spurs into his sorrel's flanks instead of his ribs.

The high-spirited horse bolted and charged down the road.

Pete couldn't help his first reaction. He sat back in the saddle and laughed at the sight of Elwin, Apache lance held high, galloping around the bend into a brush thicket and out of sight.

Piercing screams mingled with thudding hoofbeats.

"Dunny," he said to his horse, "the dude must think he sounds like a bloodthirsty Indian...oh, God, now he's yelling for help."

Pete loped to the rescue. He found Elwin jackknifed into low, thorny branches of a bare-limbed mesquite bush. He was moaning and his mount was racing for home.

Pete dismounted in one swift swinging motion and ran as fast as his tight boots would let him.

When Elwin raised his head, a thorn stabbed his left earlobe. Boots, chaps and jacket protected his body, but his face and hands were scratched and bleeding. His right arm dangled as though it had two elbows.

Flipping open the large blade of his pocket knife, Pete hacked away the thorny branches around Elwin's face. The Easterner, eyes closed, continued to moan.

"Now," said Pete, "you're free. Roll over and slide to the ground...not that way, this isn't a smooth rail fence. Roll over and get your leather chaps between you and the limbs. Come on, open your eyes; you're only a couple feet high."

Elwin slid to the ground and held his useless right arm with his left. Blood oozed and ran down his face.

"We're not far from your house, but with that broken arm, you'll have to get to a doc in town." He whacked the thorns from a limb and took out his handkerchief. "A make-do splint will have to do."

"No. You lead the horse. I'll hold myself together."

"Dammit, you have to get mounted first. Here, let me put—"

"No, no, no, no, no. I'll support my own arm."

"And I thought a mule was stubborn. All right, up you go."

Cradling his broken arm, Elwin put his left foot in the stirrup and tried to throw his other leg over the saddle. From behind, Pete tried pushing up on the dude's backside without success.

Elwin slid to the ground, groaning.

"Here, put your left foot in my hands and I'll give

you a leg up."

"I say," Elwin pleaded, "do you suppose you could have the horse kneel?"

"What do you think this is, a damned camel?"

Elwin put his foot back in the stirrup and let go his arm long enough to grab the saddle horn. With Pete pushing his rump again, he pulled himself into the seat where he settled, eyes closed, breathing hard between low moans.

Pete took reins in hand and stepped in front of his horse. "All set? Where's your lance?"

"I hope I threw it so far it joined its Apache owner."

"We have only a quarter mile to go. Can you make it?"

Elwin nodded.

Pete took a couple of steps, wriggled his toes in his tight high-heeled boots and shook his head. "I've had my horse go lame, and I've had him buck me off and get away, but this is the first time in my damned life I ever had to single-foot into headquarters leading a good, sound horse."

Gladys, arms outstretched, ran to meet them as they entered the yard. "Oh, Elllllwin!"

"He looks like he got in a fight with a wildcat and came out second best," said Pete. "His arm is broken, but the skin held."

Looking into her husband's bleeding face, Gladys asked, "Did a wildcat really do this to you?"

"No," answered Pete, tying his horse to the fence. "I was only joking about the wildcat. Elwin tried to ride a horse with no hands and ran into a few snags."

Elwin slid to the ground still holding his right arm. "I'm eternally grateful for your able assistance, but tell me, how can an Indian ride an animal and guide him with knee pressure?" He gave up on a deep-knee bend.

"I say, I pressed so hard with my legs, I have sprung joints."

Both men made snorting noises.

"You are hysterical," stated Gladys, walking between them. "The convertible is on the other side of the river, so we'll take the pickup as far as the cable car. Wait here. I'll get the truck."

"We'll come too," said Elwin. "Then we won't have to drive around by the house."

Near the barn the three stepped into the pickup and Gladys pressed the starter. At the first sound of the engine, a wild screech began in the cotton-wood tree near the irrigating pump. A dozen guinea hens ran across the corral, hens cackled, and hogs oink-oinked.

As the truck skirted the fenced pasture, a band of sheep dashed across the near field. Evidently Elwin forgot discomfort long enough to brag about the pastoral scene he had created.

"Yeah," said Pete, "but what's that horrible noise coming from the top of that cottonwood?"

"My peacock," said Gladys, proudly.

"What's he for?"

Elwin bit his lip when the truck jounced over a rut in the dirt road. "We-keep-managing-to-add-atmos-phere," he said between gasps of pain.

"You're enough atmosphere yourself," Pete said, grateful the peacock's shrill cries covered his opinion.

"Well, here we are," Gladys announced unnecessarily, as she eased the truck to a stop beside a concrete pier on the river bank. "Are you all right, dear? The cable car is waiting. Everything is working out beautifully."

Pete raised his wrinkled chin and counted the lad-der's twenty-five metal steps. He eyed the platform where a four-seat, open gondola hung from a cable by an iron pulley.

"Do you want to go first?" Gladys asked him.

He put one foot on the bottom rung, shook his head and backed away.

Gladys steadied and encouraged Elwin, as he pulled one-handed up the ladder. She followed. "Coming?" she called down.

"No," Pete answered. "I"m not going anyplace where I haven't got something between me and the ground. You two go on. The doc will fix you up." He sat on the pier and watched Gladys tug at the pull rope of the swaying cable car.

He waited until he saw them safely across the river. As they drove away in the blue convertible, Pete mumbled, "If there's a hard way to do something, a dude will think of it." Patting the concrete pier, he spoke to it as though it were alive. "Your days are numbered." He looked across the river to the gondola still swaying slightly. "And you're quite a contraption but only good until the next flood sends you, cables and all, sailing down the river."

With reluctance, he left the parked truck and walked the quarter mile back to headquarters of the Old Johnson Place. Mounting his horse he rode to the corral and put Luscombs' sick calf on green feed.

As he reined across the yard and under the gate sign which reminded him he was leaving The Wickiup, Gladys's peacock spread his long, iridescent tail and flew toward the river. *Nice shot for Elwin with his primitive lance,* he thought with a chuckle. *Poor guy. Gladys has decorated the house so full of Indian he'll be reminded of his Apache lance and wild ride even after his arm is healed up and haired over, and that won't be till Christmas.*

He settled into his saddle, "Dunny, it sure feels good

to be going home with my horse under me."

During the next few weeks Pete looked forward to Fred's school vacation visit. He and his two cowboys could use more help working the range gathering cows. There had been no fall rains.

The December day Fred came home was clear, bright, and warm. Pete greeted his son. "I'm glad you're here to help me wean the calves and give the old nellies a better chance to find what feed there is on the slopes."

Next morning they rode the south hills, staying overnight at Gonzalez's place. They worked the mountains three days before they crossed the river and joined Buzzard Ben in riding to the north.

Pete had brought Fred up to date on the doings of the Luscombs, which—except for the wild ride Elwin took with the Apache lance—didn't amount to much. It took a short visit with Ben to bring forth more news.

On December 23rd Pete, Fred, and Ben topped out and sat watching the surrounding country from the gap on Saddle Mountain. A mining town hugged the side of the hills to the west, and headquarters of four ranches were visible along the river.

Gazing down at the Old Johnson Place, Buzzard Ben chuckled. "Have you seen Elwin since he's decided he's a whole man again?"

Pete and Fred admitted they hadn't.

"He's got that tractor and 'dozer of his out diggin' dirt tanks. Says he's goin' to be ready to catch every damn drop of water when it does rain."

"He ought to get an engineer to survey and help him with the drainage," Fred began.

"Hell," said Ben, spitting as far as he could over the cliff, "he has. He's got a whole crew ahelpin' him—his own two cowboys, a soil conservation man, two government surveyors, an' a man off the county road crew."

"Depend on the dude," said Pete, "to go the whole hog."

Ben said, "It's too bad he didn't fall an' break his damned neck when he took that horseback ride Indian style. Woulda solved everythin'." He wheeled his horse. "The Luscomb women is home alone. Let's go down an' bum some lunch. With that Mexcun woman helpin' Lita an' her mom, those Eastern gals really whip up a tasty batch of groceries."

"Lita?" asked Fred.

Pete sucked in his breath. "I didn't know she planned on coming West again."

"Christmas vacation. C'mon. I'm hungry."

"Me too," said young Fred, reining off the hill after Ben.

"Not that hungry," said Pete. "I'm going to look around some more." But he didn't. He rode straight home, seething all the way.

Next day Pete worked alone. That night he confided in Pearl. "Tomorrow after we spend Christmas morning in town visiting with Fred, the girls and their families, I want to come home and take it easy. The only present I want is a nice, all-day soaking rain."

Something went wrong with Pete's plans soon after the start of the holiday. It put a damper on the day when no rain fell. Then Pete had an argument with one of his sons-in-law about religion. After a too-filling dinner, he and Pearl returned to the ranch. He was trying to settle down on the porch for a quiet rest, when Fred spun the wheels of the Ford as he drove into the yard.

"I thought that boy could drive better than that," Pete

muttered. "Must be more of that Eastern influence."

Fred bounded onto the porch. "Hi, Dad. Where's Mom?"

"Here," Pearl answered, coming from the kitchen.

"The Luscombs and their guests are coming over here for their party," he said without preliminary.

Pete jumped to his feet. "No they're not! Get out there and head them off."

"You don't understand, Dad. I invited them."

"Why?"

"Listen a minute," his son pleaded, running fingers through short-cropped hair. "I'll explain."

"Go on, son," Pearl encouraged, giving Pete a stony stare.

Fred sat on the porch ledge. "I'll get right to the point. Lita and I were discussing the tensile strength of reworked concrete. We went outside, prodded under the house to see how the foundations I helped put in were holding up. Well, to make a long story short, we poked into a sizable family of skunks. They came out from under the house and sent the guests running like flushed quail." Fred slid off the ledge. "I felt since I was responsible for breaking up the party I should ask them over."

The unmistakable sound of an approaching automobile diverted his attention. "Here comes Lita. She was right behind me. I'll run meet her. The rest of their gang will be along soon."

Pete got to his feet and said to his wife, "I'm leaving. I'm going to the outhouse." He stepped into the kitchen for a fresh bag of tobacco and a handful of matches.

Outside he met one of the women guests. She pointed to the Moore home and said, "That must be the bunkhouse. Where is your home?"

"You're looking at it," Pete answered, gritting his teeth.

"How perfectly quaint."

"Yeah," mumbled Pete, walking toward the corrals. "Us Westerners are just about the quaintest goddamned bunch of lily-livered sonsabitches on earth or we'd deport you Easterners out of Arizona and drive you to Florida like the United States Government did the renegade band of marauding Apaches."

At the corrals Pete leaned on a gatepost, looked up into a clear blue sky and spoke reverently, "God Almighty, as far as I'm concerned this isn't Jesus's birthday, and I'm not full of the spirit of loving and giving. So if it's all the same to you, I'll celebrate Christmas tomorrow."

Sheep Shearing
For A Cowboy

The first day of the new year was as cold and bleak as Pete Moore himself. He leaned on the corral fence and watched his son back out of the garage.

Fred idled the motor and called, "Dad, I know I wasn't much help to you during Christmas vacation. I'll make it up during my time off at Easter. We'll work together every day on roundup. How about it?" He gunned the motor and yelled, "Cheer up. There's nothing the matter around here a good rain wouldn't fix."

"That's what I used to think," Pete yelled. But Fred's secondhand Chevy was already down the road on the way to the university at Tucson.

The winter finally wore away, and spring was particularly welcome. In April Fred came home. He joined the roundup, and as promised worked the first day horseback. That night he ate a hearty supper of steak, beans and fried potatoes. Then, whistling all the while, he took a cold shower. Dressed in a fresh cowboy outfit, he complimented his mother's cooking, gave his father a pat on the back, and hurried out to the garage.

As the car left the yard Pete turned to Pearl. "You'd think that boy would be too tired to go to town tonight."

Pearl smiled without commenting.

Next day was a repeat of the day before. The men worked all day horseback. That night Fred bathed, shaved and, whistling as usual, drove away.

The third day Pete decided to take a little starch out of his son by getting him up an hour earlier before they took a swing around Black Mountain.

That night Pete was thoroughly exhausted, but Fred had a spring in his step as he gassed up his car.

Next morning the two men saddled their horses in the dim light of pre-dawn, rode all day and returned home after dark.

Fred's whistle was slower, but he left again after a quick supper, shower and clean clothes.

Still sitting at the table and almost too tired to talk, Pete said, "Pearl, the boy has been working like two men every day and then courting some girl in town every night. I'd say he was pretty sweet on her. Do you suppose it's that little brunette daughter of Sterns?"

"What makes you so sure the girl lives in town?"

Pete gave his wife a look from under bushy eyebrows.

"Have you noticed where the headlights come from? Or that there's fresh river mud on the wheels?"

"So the boy is doing his courting on the other side of the river." Pete tapped his spoon on the oilcloth. "Let's see, who lives over there he might be interested in?"

"Luscombs have a daughter."

Pete dropped his spoon. "She's back East."

"How do you know?"

"I guess I don't."

"Maybe she flew, but I'll bet Lita is at The Wickiup. Fred has been coming from that direction every morning lately about two o'clock."

"Two? We get up at four."

Pearl walked from the kitchen, leaving Pete alone. The only sound was an old tomcat caterwauling outside.

Next morning Pete called Fred at the usual hour. He had to call three times before the young man woke up. Looking into Fred's sleepy brown eyes, he said, "She must be quite a gal."

"She is. You wouldn't believe it."

"Come on, son," Pete said hurriedly, wanting neither to hear nor believe. He knew he had been too tired to hear his son come in. He also realized he'd been blind—blind as a man with two good eyes can be when he doesn't want to see.

On the last day before Fred had to return to his studies, he rode the full day with his father. During the afternoon, as the two men jogged along down a sand wash behind a bunch of cows and calves, Pete glanced around to see why Fred was so slow in bringing up the rear. "Hell," Pete spoke aloud, "The kid is sound asleep."

Letting the cattle walk slowly on, Pete reined around and joined Fred. "Hey," he called.

Fred's back was straight, but his head hung limp.

"Wake up."

"Huh?"

"You know, if this wasn't the last day of riding for you, you'd have to give up your working or your romancing."

Fred, his eyes clear now, grinned and took a piece of dried beef out of his shirt pocket. "I'm glad you brought that up, Dad," he said sobering. "I want to ask you a small favor." He paused. "In fact, I've already said you'd do it."

"Now Fred," warned Pete, quickly on the defensive. "You know better than to rope me into anything extra during roundup."

"This won't be any work. It's just for one evening anyway."

"Stop coyoteing around the edges and get to the point."

The young man took a deep breath. "Gladys and Elwin are taking Lita to Tucson tomorrow so that she can catch the plane. I told them you and Mother would go over and feed their stock."

"Well, you can ride over there this evening and tell them as politely I won't do any such a damn thing."

"I promised Lita."

"I don't care if you promised God Almighty. The Luscombs have two hired hands that can carry a bucket same as I can."

"They fired them last night. Sent them packing, after I said Bill and Bart were worse than useless."

Seconds slid by, measured by the cadence set by hooves of moving cattle.

"Then you do the feeding."

"But Dad, it's school for me tomorrow, too."

"All right. I know when I'm licked. I'll take care of their stock." He gave his son a scathing look before he reined sharply. "But don't expect me to climb a cottonwood tree to hand feed their damn peacock." He groaned. "I've been caught in the loop before, but this time I'm not only roped but tied."

All the way home that afternoon Pete stormed inwardly, his angry thoughts hopping around like Mexican jumping beans. *Pearl was right...the boy is sweet on Luscombs' daughter...have to feed dude*

183

stock...trapped...screwed...dammit, why didn't I admit I knew where Fred was going? Oh, oh, oh, my belly is growling again. When am I ever going to quit the damned fiddling around? Oh, God, I'm sick.

No more was said openly about the Eastern neighbors, and next day Fred drove back to school. After his son had gone, the old cowman took a short horseback ride alone.

He came home around four o'clock, and after a silent supper, backed the Ford out of the garage. Fred must have briefed his mother, because she followed him to the automobile and climbed in ready to go to the Old Johnson Place.

Pete drove across the river and three miles north. He and Pearl were greeted by demanding hunger calls from all kinds of ranch stock.

Parking the Ford near the corrals, Pete said, "You take care of the fowl and I'll feed the dairy calves and pigs."

Pete was only half through when Pearl joined him. "There's not much to do for the ducks, chickens, guinea hens, and turkeys," she said. "Elwin had self-feeders and float valves put in."

Pete closed the gate on the calves. "Then what was all the cackling I heard—the dude's stud duck missing?"

"All wanted their evening grain." Pearl set a shiny metal pail on a corner post.

There was no sound for several minutes as the noisy hogs rooted and slurped soaked barley.

Pete wiped his forehead. "We're sure having a snap of early hot weather."

His wife nodded. "By the way, the peacock didn't come up."

"Good. Maybe Elwin winged him."

The Moores left the corrals and climbed into the Ford. "We may as well feed the sissy bulls now," Pete said, "and take a turn around the pasture and check the horses."

Chores finished, they leaned on the corral fence staring into the fast-approaching dusk.

"For a man who hates sheep," Pearl said, breaking the long silence, "you're spending a lot of time looking at them."

"That old ewe there in the corner has worms."

"How do you know?"

"I might not care about the snot-noses, but I darn sure can tell when flies are laying eggs in an open wound. She must have caught her leg in some old barbed wire."

"What can you do?"

"Doctor her, same as I would a cow."

Pete went to the barn and returned carrying a coil of rope, shaking out the loop as he neared the fence. "Here, hold this bottle of medicine for me."

"Do you want me to go inside the pasture with you and head her off if you miss?"

Pete unlatched the gate. His grunt, expression, and shrug told her to join him if she so desired, but he expected to throw his loop only once.

The old cowman missed the first four throws.

Pearl, her wide print skirt flapping, made as many runs across the end of the pasture to keep the ewe turned.

When Pete missed his fifth toss, he hurled lariat aside. "It's like trying to rope a greased hog."

He and his wife ran twenty-five head into a corner where Pete made a leap and caught the ewe by one hind leg. "Bring me the bottle of screw worm medicine," he called, wrestling to hold the ewe down.

Pearl brought him the bottle of black, sticky liquid and started to open the lid.

Pete waved it aside. "That won't do, now that I think about it. That stuff will only gum up in the wool."

"So?"

"Run to the barn and see if you can find any Peerless. It's mostly alcohol and chloroform."

The ewe fidgeted and Pete fumed but held fast until Pearl returned with a bottle of clear, red liquid.

Pete sent her back to the barn two more times for more, because wool absorbed Peerless as fast as he poured it on.

"This is a losing fight, Pearl. There's bound to be an easier way of doctoring a sheep than this."

Satisfied he had done the best he could, Pete let the ewe get to her feet. The whole band of sheep, including the ether-smelling ewe, ran to the far end of the field.

Pearl toed over three empty bottles. "You put at least five dollars worth of medicine on a fifteen-dollar ewe."

"And I'd give the whole darn twenty dollars to get rid of the way I smell right now." He sniffed and made brushing motions down his chest.

"I'm surprised you offered to touch one."

"I didn't offer, but I can't let an animal suffer even if it is a sheep."

"There's a faucet at the corner of the house, but the one at the barn is closer."

"You know a little water won't take the sheep stink off a man. Soap won't help either, or gasoline." Settling himself behind the wheel of the Ford, he sighed. "No, I'll have to bury my clothes and let the smell wear off my skin. I won't be able to stand myself for a week."

As Pete spun the car out of the yard and onto the road, he said half to his wife and half to himself, "And if I don't get this dude problem settled once and for all, I won't be able to stand myself ever."

Pete wasn't at home the next evening when Gladys and Elwin called to thank him for his help. He had gone to town to see the doctor. When he returned, he threw his hat on the bed and flopped down next to it. "The doc says there's nothing the matter with me except worry and maybe smoking too much."

Pearl smoothed his head at the temples. "It's not like you to make yourself sick over what's been or what's to be."

Pete raised on one elbow. "Easterners would get anybody steamed up. With them around, I can't get settled."

His wife pulled up a chair and sat close to the bed. "The Luscombs were here. They left about an hour ago. They were thankful to us for feeding the animals. Elwin said he didn't mind about all the medicine you used. He was pleased that you'd do it for him."

"I didn't."

"Gladys said she hoped she wasn't imposing on such helpful neighbors, but they have to return to Tucson next week to bring out two new cowboys they hired."

Pete stared in silence at the dark, brown ceiling.

Pearl didn't falter in her line of talk. "They don't expect us to care for their stock. They will leave early in the morning this time and come home do chores, but—"

"But what?" interrupted Pete, rolling over on his side.

"The day they leave is the only time they can get the sheep shearer to come out. I told them we'd go over and wait for the man."

"This is too much."

"We don't have to do anything but sit. The house is nice, and I know it would make Fred happy."

"Does it matter any more if I'm happy?"

"You don't have to go. I will. I promised." Her voice was as soft and caressing as a cool spring breeze, when she added, "They would do as much for you."

"That would be even worse. The only thing I ask of a dude is to leave me and mine alone." He sighed again and turned over, right arm thrown across his cowboy hat, and said no more.

In spite of his stated feelings, Pete went with Pearl to the Old Johnson Place on the appointed day and waited for the sheep shearer. As he knew he would, he got roped into helping.

Wrangling and saddling one of Elwin's horses, he told his wife, "At least I'm going to do what part of this damn job I can horseback. I'll drive the sheep to the shed. You're free to make the shearer a hand if you want to."

The three were starting work on the last bunch when there came a rattle of hoofs and a familiar voice taunting, "Uh, oh." Buzzard Ben, reined his horse to the side of the shed. "Don't I know you, cowboy?"

Caught stacking fleece, Pete kept his head down.

Ben leaned over the saddlehorn and jeered, "Petey had a little lamb, little lamb, little lamb. Why, I do believe this is the very same cowboy that gave me such a razzin' for diggin' up dead Injuns for a dude woman. I know what I was doin' it for. What are you after?"

"You can see we're busy. We'll thresh this out later."

The shearer, straddling a sheep, waved clippers. "We're almost done but could use another hand on the windup."

Ben threw back his head and laughed a long, raucous laugh. "Rather take a beatin'."

"So would I," Pete echoed. "This is it. This is the end."

Ship One, Ship All

Pete rubbed his bald head, looked at the kitchen calendar on the wall and then back to Buzzard Ben sitting opposite. "Tomorrow is May 13th. Friday the 13th, and it's shipping day."

"You've already said that three times," his neighbor answered, "Let me tell you how I got the day figured."

"I don't know why I ever agreed to such a crazy scheme."

"You agreed because that fast-talkin' Colorado cattle buyer sold you, that's why." Ben chuckled.

Pete ground his cigarette butt into a Mason jar lid. "I shouldn't have said I'd deliver so early, and I shouldn't have agreed to deliver to the same shipping point with a dude."

"Don't forget Gonzalez will be there."

"All of us trying to drive and corral our yearlings at the same time. It'll be the damndest mix-up you ever saw when four of us try to sort cattle and load out from that dinky little Southern Pacific stockyard in town. It'd be bad enough with just you and me. I

189

hate to think about Gonzalez and Elwin Luscomb crossing the river together and joining us." Pete teetered on the back legs of his chair and shook his head. "I told that buyer we couldn't do it in the first place, but he said if he didn't get the cattle on pasture in Colorado by next week there'd come a snow before they were on grass sixty days."

"Hold on," Ben said. "Change of plan. Since me an' Gonzalez sold by the head, we don't need scales. We're takin' the upper crossing and'll be ahead of you and Elwin. I'll corral first. I don't know where the rest of you'll be, but Elwin will have to cool his heels outside the corrals until the train crew gets my yearlin's loaded."

Pete leaned across the table. "You don't suppose Elwin will have an asthma attack tomorrow, do you?"

"So his wife and the cowboys could deliver alone?" Ben laughed. "Hell no! Gladys wouldn't miss the show, an' Elwin won't fold that early in the game."

"Of all the money he's spent, he hasn't decent corrals and no scales."

Ben's raucous laughter ended in chuckling and coughing. "That's why I told him it would be simple to use yours."

"You didn't!"

"Why not? It's neighborly."

"I ought to skin you alive and tack your hide to the barn door."

Ben jumped to his feet, overturning his chair. "Don't you threaten me, Pete Moore."

The old cowman cradled his bald head in his arms. "Who can a man trust? I wish it was tomorrow and shipping day was over. Then I'd be on my way to the line camp in the hills with a good two-week's supply of food."

Buzzard Ben righted his chair and left without saying another word.

Pete, his head still lowered, pounded the table with both fists. "And Fred says he can't leave school this year to help."

Before dawn next day, while Pete was gathering cattle out of fields for early-morning weighing, he heard a loud "Ki-yi-yippie" at the river crossing. Galloping to investigate, he found Elwin and two cowboys driving the Luscombs' yearlings. The Easterner loped ahead and boasted, "See I can get up early."

Pete's chin dropped toward his open collar. "How did you gather out of your fields and drive three miles by now?"

Elwin reared his mount to a stop. "I held them in the corrals all night. Good planning, right?"

Pete groaned, realizing the man had already shrunk at least sixty pounds off his steers and heifers by giving them a twelve-hour stand before weighing.

Elwin's voice rose in triumph. "My wife will be along later in the truck. After Ben said you offered to let me use your scales, I thought it would be so much simpler for us to pool our cowboys and cattle and drive to town together."

Before Pete could protest, he was distracted by the sound of an approaching automobile. "Hold on. Here comes the buyer."

Paying no attention to his herd, Elwin reined around and galloped to meet the oncoming car.

Cursing under his breath, Pete returned to his men and the task of driving yearlings out of fields and corralling them next to the scales.

Two hours later both Moores' and Luscombs' cattle were sorted, weighed, and ready to be driven ten miles to the shipping point. Gonzales had not yet come down from the south hills with his bunch, and Buzzard Ben had driven his on ahead.

At eight o'clock Elwin shouted words he had heard or read. Dropping his "th's", he sang out, "C'mon, boys, let's head 'em up and move 'em out."

"Not time yet," Pete answered.

The buyer drove his four-door sedan across the river to watch for Gonzalez. Pete left the corral and went to the house for another cup of coffee. "Pearl, this is supposed to be the happiest day of the year." He held his hands over his stomach. "And I'm sick as a poisoned dog."

His wife filled two white enamelware cups. "It'll work out," she said, pulling the sugar bowl closer.

Pete stirred and blew on hot coffee. After two slurps, he said, "Got to get back. No telling what Elwin will think of next. I don't know which is worse—having him out of sight with me worrying about what he's up to, or having him underfoot where I get in the middle of his messes."

He gulped and swallowed twice before getting to his feet and starting for the door. "Got to get back."

Pearl smiled. "Go on, and stop repeating yourself."

When Pete returned to the corral, the cowboys were sitting on the fence. They were quiet, smoking and waiting. Elwin alone was active. He was trying to load a yearling into his pickup. Behind the wheel, Gladys jockeyed their truck until the tailgate was flush with the top of the chute.

High on the loading platform, one of Elwin's cowboys held the tailgate and waited for the steer to be pushed into the back of the truck.

Elwin, arms wide, hollered and made kicking motions with his right foot, as the steer turned and started back down the chute.

Running forward, Pete called, "What in the hell are you trying to do?"

Elwin stopped kicking and looked down. "The buyer refused this little steer because of small size. We'll take him to Tucson for locker beef." The Easterner raised his foot to push the animal's rump into the truck bed.

Without warning the steer whirled, stuck his head between Elwin's legs and ducked down the chute, Elwin riding the neck backward.

Pete climbed on the fence in time to see the steer make the turn at the bottom of the chute and buck off across the corral. Elwin was hanging on when the steer passed the squeeze chute, raced through an open gate and past the manger.

Gladys set the brake and slid from the cab. Bosom bouncing, red hair flying, she ran crying, "Oh, Elllllwin."

Pete blinked and craned his neck to see into the next corral. The steer, with Elwin now lying almost flat along his back, ran into the far fence and fell in a heap. The dude rolled clear and sat in swirling dust clouds.

All hands rallied. The cowboy nearest the "wreck" slid off the fence and helped the dazed Easterner to his feet. "That was every bit as good as professional bull riding in the big time, with a repeat performance of an evening."

Elwin slapped fine dirt from his clothing. "I don't know what I did, but I'm positive I couldn't do it again."

Pete agreed. "Nobody could again." Grabbing the now docile steer by an ear with his right hand, he twisted the steer's tail with his left. Grunting, the old cowman half-led, half-pushed the animal back through two corrals and up the loading chute.

Thump! The steer's weight hit the truck bed. Pete

grabbed the end gate. Fastening bolts, he said, "Now unless we can think of some more delaying action, we'll drive these damn cattle to the stockyards."

Maybe Elwin was bruised, but he hadn't hurt himself enough to keep him from riding horseback. All the way to town he rode his horse around cattle, in front of cattle, and behind cattle. He cut the bunched herd into two sections and almost ran a dozen head back to Moores' headquarters in his attempt to turn them.

"Elwin," yelled Pete, veins swelling in his neck, "for Chri'sake, get the hell off to one side and watch getaway places." Relieved the ten-mile drive was nearly over, he shook sweat from his forehead and regrouped the cattle.

Rounding the last curve in the road, Pete turned and reined close to his Eastern neighbor. "We've almost got it made. Take it easy here," he pleaded. "There's about fifteen-hundred people in this little burg, and they'll come out to see if we can get these yearlings across the pavement, through the edge of town, and into the pens. Easy now. Don't make any quick moves."

Cowboys flanked the herd and brought up the rear, as Pete rode ahead to point the lead. Experience had taught him the tricky business of knowing when to check the forward movement and when not to. Because the drive had to go part way up the street, turn left, cross the railroad tracks, and go another hundred yards to the pens, he looked ahead at the bare, deserted street. Furtively, his eyes slid past a garage, two stores, a bar, and a barber shop. People peeked from parked cars and open windows.

Twisting around in the saddle, Pete watched the oncoming herd from thirty feet in the lead. Wary cattle, heads low, rolled their eyeballs and sniffed the pavement. Their steady hoofbeats were slow and rhythmical.

Pete noticed a small animal poke his nose up and make a dodging movement. Before he could get a cry of warning across his lips, Elwin jumped his horse out from the side. When his mount's hooves hit the pavement, they slipped. Horse and rider fell. Elwin pulled the reins and held on. His mount gathered himself and stumbled to his feet, but the damage was done.

Cattle, already half-frightened by the strangeness of town, broke herd and ran in all directions. A third galloped straight at Pete, who loped ahead.

For the next ten minutes there was utter confusion. Tails high, cattle ran all over town, bawling and dodging.

Cursing in both English and Spanish, Pete signalled his men and together they went to work regathering.

An hour later he and two of his cowboys rode back into town from the east driving about fifty head. Buzzard Ben joined them. "Where in hell have you been all mornin'? I've had my cattle in the pens for three hours."

Pete stood in his stirrups and gazed around. "And it's liable to take me three days."

"The Colorado cattle buyer got here a while ago, an' Gonzalez drove easy through town. He's got his yearlin's in the corrals now with mine."

"Yeah," Pete commented. "I had the easiest drive to the yards, but here I am loose herding my own yearlings outside with a dude." He frowned, adding, "I haven't got them all either."

By noon the Moore and Luscomb cattle were counted and standing in a sand wash on the west side of the stockyards.

Ben asked, "Get 'em all back?"

Pete finished rolling a cigarette. "Hell no! I've driven cattle over here every year I've delivered, and I've never had a road loss. This year I'm five head short." He stared at the milling herd and listened for the first, faint chugging of an approaching train. "And they aren't loaded yet."

Elwin rode a slow pace to greet his neighbors. "I say, I had no idea I would cause a stampede when I—"

"Forget it," Pete said, cutting short the apology before taking a long drag on his smoke.

Inside the stockyards the cattle inspector had finished counting, sorting and writing down brands. Gonzalez and Ben sat on the fence and made their own check counts. Pete, Elwin, and their men, continued circling horseback in order to keep cattle on the outside bunched and quieted.

The train rounded a curve and chugged to a stop, the side of one of the cattle cars spotted in front of the loading chute. There was plenty of help in the work following. It was a noisy operation, with cowboys pushing, shoving, kicking and cursing—their high-pitched "Hi-ya, hi-ya, hi-yas" mingling with cattle bawls and trumpet-like bellows. Metal bars clinked and wooden boards rattled while pungent smells of fresh-dropped manure filled the air and gray, gritty dust enveloped the scene.

Pete, still horseback in the open with his unfenced cattle, leaned forward watching neighbors' cattle loaded. One by one slatted cars lurched forward, were loaded and moved on. From the near side of the chute, brakeman made waving motions to the engineer each time the train moved the necessary number of feet. The engineer gave answering signals by blowing his whistle. Every time the whistle tooted, yearlings raised heads and made darting movements.

Finally Ben's and Gonzalez's yearlings were loaded, and Pete and Elwin drove their cattle into the yards. Wiping his forehead, Pete rode over to Buzzard Ben. "I never was so damn glad to corral a bunch in my life. Between the engineer hanging on that whistle, and Elwin trotting around on his bay horse, I had a picture of my cattle running to Mexico instead of being shipped to Colorado. And with the chousing around they've had this morning, I'm glad as hell they're weighed."

Ben tied his horse to the fence and climbed over into the corral. "I just seen Gonzalez acomin' this way with three of the five you're short."

Pete rode through the corral and out the gate to help. Elwin beat him. Smiling, the Easterner reined around and with prancing horse joined Gonzalez. They drove three head into the corral.

Closing the gate, Pete turned to Gonzalez. From the corner of tight-pressed lips he said, "The greenhorn caused the whole mess in the first place, and now he's claiming credit for these you found." Still fuming, he returned to the loading chute to help count, sort, and load his steers and heifers.

Cowboy calls and cattle bawling began again, together with whistles and rattles, as the operation was repeated.

When the last bull bar was placed across the open side of the car, the train pulled ahead and the wing gates on the chute slid back. Bone weary, Pete's knees threatened to buckle, as he limped over to where Buzzard Ben sat on the fence.

Ben grinned. "Except for two head, you're gettin' shipped."

"And did you ever see a sloppier job? It's a hell of

a way to wind up a season. My son will take over the ranch next year, and I'll have this." His right arm circled overhead in a roping motion, as though he expected to catch the whole scene in his loop. "This is my final shipping day."

Elwin and Gonzalez started walking across the corral, as Pete and Ben slid off the fence.

"Wouldja look at those two bein' almost buddy-buddy," Ben said.

"Yeah," Pete agreed. "It looks like the Mexican got over thinkin' our Eastern neighbor was out to paw his wife."

"You know, Elwin's a hell of a good sport. Don't hold no grudges neither."

The four men met at the gate.

"We made it," Elwin said.

"*We* sure did," agreed Ben, giving Pete an elbow dig in the ribs.

Gonzalez smoothed both sides of his moustache. "Time to eat now, yes? A beeg steak?"

"I say," interjected Elwin. Picking up a metal prod pole from between the corral rails, he held it out. "I saw men jabbing cattle and pushing them up the chute with this."

"You sure did," agreed Ben. "That's a hot shot. There's batteries inside the tube an' a hot wire with 60 volts." Grabbing it from Elwin's hand, he continued, "When a cow brute won't move, you jab it in the rear like this." Ben touched the hot shot against the seat of Elwin's pants. There was *zzst-zzst* sound and a yelp from the dude as he leaped high in the air.

Onlookers chuckled and cheered.

Ben bent double with laughter. "Elwin, you got the legs of a hop toad."

"And just about as much sense," Pete mumbled.

The Easterner started to walk off, changed direction, rejoined the group and laughed with them. "I'm hungry, too. Shall we proceed in orderly fashion to the restaurant?"

"I'm riding home," Pete said. "My belly feels full of rocks."

"That's your head arattlin'," Ben said.

Elwin brushed at a smear of dust on his shirt pocket and then motioned to Gladys, perched atop a stockyard gate, to join the group. He made eye contact with Pete. "I say, we're having a party this evening at The Wickiup. Later we plan to show the film Ben took last fall when we went on that wild-horse chase."

Pete's voice faltered. "You, you mean you really got pictures?"

Ben nodded. "I didn't get anything of the Luscombs catching horses, but I got some dandy shots of 'em running down their own mounts and then losin' 'em—never shoulda unsaddled even for a picture."

Elwin smiled. "After awhile one laughs at one's mistakes."

"Better come take a look," Ben urged.

"No thanks," Pete said as he untied his horse. "I have business to attend to in the mountains."

There was a flurry of activity, as the cowboys mounted and Gladys slid behind the wheel of her truck.

Pete did not join the fun and hullabaloo that always followed shipping day but let his horse trot most of the way back to headquarters.

He spent two hours loading his pack mule, pleased he had persuaded Pearl to stay in town with their youngest daughter and family.

Riding southwest toward the hills, he turned in the saddle and spoke to the mule at the end of the lead rope. "Come on, you long-eared old jackass. We're going up where the air is clear and untouched by dudes—where a man can think and figure things out for himself."

Out Of The Blue

The June day Pete came home from his stay in the mountains Buzzard Ben was waiting for him horseback by the gate at Moores' headquarters. "Hello, Pete," he said. "You look like a damned ol' prospector with all them whiskers an' that pack mule. You been sulkin' in the hills three weeks. Sure you didn't stake out a claim?"

The old cowman shook his head. "Nope, but I found peace an' quiet. No trouble and no dudes."

Ben chuckled. "Well, it's a good thing you're rested. You're comin' back to plenty of both."

"Don't mention it now."

The two rode to the corrals. "It's hot early," Pete said, "and we need a rain."

"I know. I waited here to tell you about Elwin's plans."

"Do we have to talk about him?" Pete stormed. "I've spent over two weeks getting the poisoning out of my system, and first thing I hear when I get back is news of Elwin Luscomb."

"Yes, we do," answered Ben, dismounting. "We got to talk about rain, and, as it happens, he is in the big fat middle of our rain problem."

Pete scratched his bearded face and leaned over the horse's neck. "I suppose he's taking care of everything?" Sarcasm curled the edges of his words.

"That's what he claims."

Pete swung off his horse and began unpacking the mule.

"What are you getting at?"

Ben untied leather straps and unloaded the opposite side. "To start with, Elwin went and bought rain gauges an' put 'em up all over the range. Hell, he must've put out couple a dozen—two kinds, one's a little glass tube, the other, a funnel with a bucket underneath. There's a glass one on your front gatepost."

Pete looked over the mule's back at his neighbor. "He figures God Almighty will be accommodating and fill them up tomorrow?"

"Oh, Elwin figures on helpin'."

"When are we going to measure all this rain?"

"Be patient. That's what the dude says."

"My patience is worn pretty thin right now," Pete said, pulling the pack saddle into his arms. Holding the weight on one hip, he started for the barn. "I've known for the two years he's been here, that lawyer is never going to be a cowboy, but I did give him credit for having common horse sense."

"You're the only man around here that's real smart, huh?"

"No, but I have some smarts."

"You haven't got as much sense as this mule, and you could teach it a thing or two about bein' stubborn." He handed over the lead rope and mounted his horse.

"S'long," he called, tugging his wide hat brim.

Pete mounted, put the mule in the corral, and reined toward the house. Home now, his horse fought turning away from the barn, but Pete anticipated seeing his wife and, with a light touch of his spurs, trotted across the yard.

That weekend the Moores went to the University of Arizona to see Fred graduate. Pete had looked forward to attending the ceremony, but when the time came, feelings of satisfaction were smothered by a sense of loss he was unable to understand. Turning over the reins of running the ranch to his son was going to be more difficult than he anticipated, even though he felt it was necessary. Was his life work over? Finished? Done? He clutched his stomach, wondering why he felt so sick.

Although he tried, he couldn't find Fred among the sea of seated, black-robed graduates. Later he recognized his son by his rolling gait across the stage and arm-roping motion when he reached up and flipped the mortar board tassel.

Pete turned and looked at Pearl. Eyes brimming with tears, the parents smiled at each other.

Next morning Pete greeted Fred at the breakfast table. "Son, it's sure good to have you home. You'll want to rest up, but I know you've lots of plans for running the ranch." He stood in the doorway and rubbed his fingers around his hat brim. "I'll go up to Gonzalez's today and fix up the deed on that water right we traded for. I want you to know you've got the go-ahead with me. I trust your judgment."

"Thanks, Dad."

Pete walked to the corral and saddled his favorite mount.

"Dunny," he said, "I've turned myself out to pasture. I'm a used-up old work horse."

Leaning with his head against his mount's strong neck, he didn't hear the first sounds of an approaching motor. When he did pay attention and raise his head, the pulsing roar was almost on him. "My Lord!" he cried, as a low-flying biplane dipped over headquarters and waggled its wings. The chickens squawked as they ran for cover. Pete held the reins of his rearing horse.

The roar lessened. Leading Dunny, Pete joined Pearl in the open clearing between house and corrals. "Who do you suppose that darn fool is?"

"A crop-dusting airplane from the valley?"

Pete didn't notice the teasing tone of his wife's voice. He let his gaze follow the plane as it flew southeastward. "You don't suppose Elwin is spending three dollars an acre to spray insecticide on that sixty acres of weedy pastureland?"

Pearl tucked a long strand of hair into the bun at the nape of her neck.

Chickens quieted. Dunny stopped quivering.

Pete mounted. "Why did that plane come over here wagging its wings?" Waving goodbye, he called, "Gonzalez is expecting me, so I won't be long. Home tomorrow night."

As he rode across the river, he mused, "That's funny. Fred didn't come out of the house. I wonder where he is and if there is something going on I don't know about."

When Pete returned from Gonzalez's place, the night was hot, close and sultry the way it usually was before a storm. Pearl moved their bed out onto the screened porch where they could catch any breath of air that stirred. Fred was not at home, and Pete felt as befuddled as an owl in daylight.

By the time he woke up, sun was in his eyes. Both wife and son were gone without explanation.

That afternoon he leaned against the barn and watched the same low-flying biplane. It flew up and down the river at least half dozen times, making wide circles, tight circles and passes over the hills before it disappeared over the mountains.

About thirty minutes after the plane left, Fred rode to the corral and swung off his horse. "Hi, Dad. You're slumped over again. Didn't get your sleep out? When I left this morning you were snoring. Did you get everything fixed up with Gonzalez?"

Pete nodded. "Where is your mother?"

"Drove the Ford to Luscombs'."

"Are you going to stand there unsaddling your horse without saying a word about that airplane?"

The young man didn't answer. He grinned at his father before he ducked his head and unbuckled the flank cinch.

"Do you know something about the low-flying plane?"

"Sure."

"What's it all about?"

Fred pulled off his saddle and carried it into the barn. "I wasn't going to say anything for a few days until we are more positive of the results."

Following behind his son, Pete said, "You were brought up on a horse. Don't tell me you're cowboying in an airplane."

"No, it's an experiment." After lifting his saddle to a rope hanging from a rafter and slipping a loop around the horn, Fred continued. "I know you won't like the idea at first, but you told me to go ahead." He ran his fingers through his short-cropped hair.

"We want to give this theory a try before you pass judgment."

"We?"

"Elwin and I."

The cowman turned on his boot heel. "You're right. If you have a scheme cooked up with that dude, I don't want to hear it." He walked across the yard and into the house, feeling like a tired, old, beaten jackass.

Next morning Pete woke up before dawn and fumbled around under the bed for his boots.

Pearl stirred. "Are you leaving before breakfast?"

"I'll be back. I'm going to take a little sashay up river. When Fred gets up, tell him he caught me snoring once, but snow will fall in hell before he beats his old man up again."

Half an hour later he rode up the side of the river. It was barely daylight when he heard faint clop-cloppings of an approaching horse.

"Hello, Ben," he said minutes later.

"Hello yourself. There's a cow hidin' there in the brush. I'm followin' her back to her wormy calf. What are you doin'?"

"Hunting you."

Ben took cigarette makings from his pocket. "Well, you found me. What's on your mind?"

Reining close, Pete leaned on the pommel of his saddle. "What the hell is an airplane doing here on the river?"

"Didn't Fred tell you?"

"I wouldn't listen."

"You shoulda. Maybe you coulda talked him outa the idea."

"Fred's or Elwin's?"

"Both, I guess. They're hepped on the idea of makin' rain. Scientific, too." Ben waved his arms. "I tried to tell you when you come home from the hills, but you was so damned stubborn I figured I may as well save my breath and let you find out for yourself."

"If you'd ever come right out and say anything instead of teasing me along like a cat with a mouse, maybe I'd listen better. Now what the hell is going on around here?"

Ben let his voice drop back to normal speaking level. "There is some kind of theory that if rain clouds won't spill over, a man can spray 'em with stuff they call silver iodide." Ben peered closely at his neighbor. "Do you follow me?"

"So far."

"Then, I don't exactly get this next part myself, but Elwin says.... Now wait, I'll remember, yeah, he says, 'Moisture from the clouds condenses and forms water particles on this here core of silver iodide'." Ben circled one forefinger around the other. "When the drops get heavy they fall, and there's your rain."

Pete snorted.

"Go ahead. Say it's hogwash. I don't know why I bother answerin' you anyway." He smacked reins against chaps and snickered. "I bet that middle-aged dude flies aroun' in that plane seedin' clouds like he was a young man sewing his wild oats."

"Sounds plumb loco."

"Ask Fred," said Ben, his voice rising to a shout. "He read it to me. Showed me figures—proof of government experiments."

"Wait a damn minute. I thought you said it was Elwin's idea."

"Tryin' it out here was. Fred an' Lita was talkin', an' the dude decided to give the idea a go on the river."

"Lita?"

"Sure. Don't you know she's back?"

"Yeah...yeah...that is...not yet, I guess." Touching spurs to his horse's sides, Pete said, "Thanks for the information. Got to go. Promised Pearl I'd be home for breakfast."

"You mean you ain't had your usual bacon and eggs yet? Go on an' get your belly full before Fred tells you what sprayin' the clouds is goin' to cost you."

Pete reined sharply. "Cost who?"

"They tried to get me in on it, but I told 'em I wasn't payin' no three-hundred dollars for a 'maybe' rain."

"Isn't Elwin financing the deal?"

"I guess he's footin' most of the bill, since his ranch pool fell through. I told him I wouldn't chip in a damned dime. He admitted las' night that Gonzalez throwed him out on his ear."

"Anybody else helping?"

"Nobody but your son." Ben took up his reins. "There goes my cow. Thinks she's givin' me the slip, but I'm on her tail."

Pete's shoulders slumped. "I'm more mixed up than ever, but thanks for telling me about the airplane. Need any help?"

"Naw, go eat your breakfast. I pretty much know where the ol' nellie has her calf hid out, and it ain't far."

Without another word Pete turned and rode toward home.

It was sunup when he tied his horse to the fence, slammed the gate shut, and stamped into the house.

"Right on time for breakfast," Pearl said, turning thick-sliced bacon in a black cast-iron skillet.

"Where's Fred?"

"Feeding the horses."

"Did you know that boy paid Elwin three-hundred dollars to shoot silver iodine into clouds?"

"Iodide, not iodine," Pearl corrected, flipping hot grease over two eggs.

"Why didn't you tell me?"

"Better to show you. Maybe rain will come from the cloud seeding today."

"Maybe it will rain anyway."

"Sit down and eat," suggested Pearl, as she dished up her husband's plate. "Fred will be in. Remember, you said he could take over running the ranch and you'd trust him to use his own ideas."

"Not in cahoots with Elwin."

"That's his judgment."

Pete slumped in his chair. "Ben told me Lita is back at the Old Johnson Place. Did you know?"

When his wife simply nodded, Pete gobbled up an egg in two bites and jabbed his fork into a strip of bacon. "It sure makes a man feel good to have to ask the neighbors what his own family is doing."

"Shush. Here's Fred. Please don't badger him. Wait until this afternoon. You'll see."

Pete greeted his son, gulped two more bites, and with a biscuit in hand called over his shoulder, "Got to go."

He mounted and left horseback, hating the thought of his son being part of a harebrained idea. And hearing about it second hand was galling.

Mid-afternoon he rode out of the south hills toward home. It was unusually warm for late June, even in the foothills. Overhead the sky was a clear blue with some drifting white puffs.

The only possible rain cloud was a mass gathering over Gonzalez's range.

The faint hum of a motor broke the silence. As the sound grew louder, Pete stopped his horse atop a knoll overlooking the river. An airplane circled the Old

Johnson Place, winged over the San Pedro River and gave the Moore headquarters a buzzing. Then it began diving into puffy white clouds.

From watching the plane soar in and out of sight, Pete got a crick in his neck. Disgusted he rode homeward, sure in his own mind if Elwin and Fred expected water to fall from the sky, they had better fly up with two buckets full and pour it out of the plane.

Almost home, he noticed a low-hanging haze over the river. He thought he smelled rain. By the time he reached the crossing, he was sure of the unmistakable odor of moisture on dust and dry creosote bushes. The ground was damp, and the whole riverbed had the fresh-washed look of a travel poster. A few frogs along the banks croaked hopefully.

Pete crossed the shallow stream and rode into headquarters. Fred and the Luscomb family galloped to meet him. They shouted in unison, "It worked!"

Pete stopped his horse at the gate. "How do you know?"

"Can't you smell the rain?" Fred asked.

"Didn't you see it?" added Lita.

"It is the most remarkable thing Elwin has ever done," Gladys bragged.

Elwin motioned to the glass gewgaw mounted on Moores' front yard post. "Here's the proof." Dismounting, he ran an index finger along the red calibrated lines. "Seven-one-hundredths of an inch, as close as I can tell."

"Not much of a rain," Pete remarked, whispering under his breath, "A hummingbird can piss more than that."

"We'll do better next month when we have heavier clouds, Daddy says," Lita added.

"And you all take bows?"

"Fred and the pilot deserve most of the credit," Elwin said, perhaps hesitant to include himself in the loop of praise.

After swinging back into his saddle, he continued, "Don't worry. When clouds refuse to give up their moisture, we shall force them to release their life-giving droplets."

Pete shifted his boots in the stirrups. "I believe a man can string along with nature and get along fine, but when he goes to forcing he runs into trouble."

"Come on, Dad," Fred spoke up. "The West is growing and changing. This is progress."

Elwin beamed. "I say, the plane is over at The Wickiup. Have you ever seen your ranch from the air?"

"No, and I never will. Saddle high is as far up as I intend to go."

Fred, heading for the river crossing, called over his shoulder, "Come on, Lita. Let's check the rain gauge down at the Mexican's truck garden."

After they left, Gladys said, "Dear, we must hurry home and do our chores. Bye-bye. Oh, this is all so exciting."

Elwin took one last proud look at the drop of rain in the glass tube and followed as his wife galloped off.

Pete didn't want to hear any more about scientific rain, but Fred and Pearl talked of nothing else all next day.

Rain talk continued that evening when Gonzalez showed up at Moores' headquarters. He made his position clear, closing his eyes to narrow slits and fingering his opened knife blade. "First, Mr. Luscomb try to steal my wife. Now my beautiful cloud."

Pete motioned for his neighbor to sit on the extra porch chair. "How did he steal your cloud?"

Fred stepped out onto the porch. "I don't believe Elwin would steal anything."

Gonzalez raised eyelids a fraction and pushed his face close to Fred's. "You are part of this rain? You shoot the cloud, no?"

"Yes, but..."

"But you not know where rain she will fall?"

"No, I mean yes, we don't know within a radius of miles. Considering the drift and wind, plus the factor of...."

"*Bastante!* All day this cloud she stay over my rancho. Rain will come. I know it. I feel it. Here." Gonzalez pounded his chest. "Then you dive airplane into my cloud, back and down, and up, like this." He raised his knife and sliced the air. "My beeg, beautiful cloud break, go down river...fall to your rancho." He included Pete in his scathing glance.

"Don't look at me," the old cowman protested. "I'm no rainmaker."

"It will average out," Fred said, voice placating. "Next time our cloud will spill on your place."

Gonzalez snapped his knife closed. "Is good. I go now to *Elena.*" Again narrowing his eyes to slits he pocketed and patted his knife. "No more airplane over my rancho. I no like to have nothing steal from me."

After he had gone Fred said, "Whew. I thought we had things patched up, but he's jealous about everything. Is he really that serious?"

Pete refused to become part of the problem. "You and Elwin will have to swear in another witness."

Fred nodded. "I'm going out to the barn. Want to help me load salt blocks? The deer on Black Mountain are sure getting in their licks—no pun intended. What do you think?"

Pete realized his son expected no answer. He was already on the way to the corrals, uninterested in listening to his father worry about being caught in the loop with Easterners and their harebrained ideas.

Duded Out

Early one morning toward the end of June, Pete pulled on his clothes, reached for his Stetson, and slipped out the back door of his ranch house. Back bent, feet dragging, he walked to the barn near the corrals. Unwilling to admit being sorely troubled, he convinced himself he simply wanted to take advantage of cool air to shoe one of his mounts.

Inside, the building smelled of hay, sweat-soaked leather, and linseed oil. After he pulled on his chaps to protect his legs, he reached into a salvaged oil drum and scooped rolled barley into a morral made from a burlap sack. Carrying the knotted end over his arm, he opened the corral gate, stepped inside and closed it, careful to hide the bridle held behind his back. Right arm extended, he shook the sack of feed as he walked toward the lone horse standing in a far corner.

"Come on, boy," he coaxed.

The dun-colored gelding whirled, snorted, kicked his hind legs and ran past the old cowman to the opposite corner of the corral.

Slowly, Pete turned and approached the horse again. The animal whinnied, took two mincing steps before shaking his mane, swishing his tail, and galloping to another corner.

With no show of impatience and without raising his voice, Pete shook the morral and eased toward the horse. "Here, boy."

The animal nickered and stood, head raised, nostrils flared, while Pete walked one easy step at a time until man and beast met.

The horse lowered his head and nuzzled into the feed bag, apparently unmindful of the knotted strap sliding down his mane and settling on his neck.

For several minutes there was no sound but grind and crunch of chewing. Tossing his head in an attempt to flip the last of the rolled barley into his mouth, the animal was helped by his owner, who pushed the bottom of the burlap feeder upward. "That's it," Pete said, taking empty sack into his arm with a continuing motion that eased bridle into place. A handful of flattened grain dribbled from the horse's lips when Pete, thumb first, pried open his mouth and slid the bit across teeth and over tongue. Ears twitched when the headstall touched the horse.

Pete led his mount out of the corral and tied reins to one of the shed's posts. "Dunny, when a man can't figure the answers, he'd better put his head down, his ass up and let his mind wander."

He put a wooden box of farrier's tools on the ground a yard away. Then he stood alongside the horse, took off his sweat-stained cowboy hat and put it near his feet. He placed his near hand on the horse's hip before he picked up the foot and placed it across his thigh. With pinchers he pulled the old shoe. Using hoof cutter and rasp, he proceeded to trim and reshape the hoof. The procedure was much the same as a person manicuring long fingernails.

As he worked, mental pictures and bits of conversation floated in and out of memory. It had been the same time in June on a similar day. Moores' yearlings had been shipped, ranch work had settled into the usual routine, and it was time for making next year's plans. He and Fred were riding horseback through underbrush along the San Pedro River. Pete remembered how he had peered into the thicket and pretended to be casual as he asked, "Have you been thinking about what I said about taking an engineering course when you go back to school?"

Fred's answer was a noncommittal, "I've been thinking."

When his son didn't continue, Pete recalled the argumentative edge his voice took when he said, "Those agricultural courses are fine, but they're too damn full of theory. A man's got to learn his own land, and they don't teach you that out of books. This marginal cattle range will run ten cows to the section. Some say it'll run fifteen. You and I know it won't. Nowadays it takes more than being a cattleman to run an outfit. The West is outgrowing me. I don't want it to outgrow you."

Pete remembered how easily Fred had moved in the saddle, listening and nodding. "I've always been able to hold my own with cattle buyers, but you should have been here this spring. There I was at the kitchen table with a pencil stub and lined tablet. I darn near fainted when that dressed up, fast-talking fellow pulled a slide rule out of his briefcase. He quoted me a contract price on the cows and calves separate before I could put a number on paper."

Fred's response had been, "Yeah, Dad, I'm looking forward to trying some of my ideas here—soil erosion, permanent pastures, and reseeding."

Pete recalled the exact words of his answer: "The hell with ideas! You can't run a cattle ranch with ideas. If you don't learn how to operate your outfit on a paying basis, the whole Southwest is going to the damn dudes. They're coming in with their money, buying up ranches all around and taking cattle raising business out of the hands of cowmen."

Dropping his horse's hoof and returning to the present, Pete shouted, "Dunny, that son of mine called it progress. That's exactly what he said, 'Dad, it's Progress.' I call it ruination. Those greenhorns will get tired of the grind. When the newness wears off, they'll quit—lots of them will—and what have they done to us? Built a lot of fancy houses and invested in frills that ups the price of the land so the natives can't go out and get a working unit to raise beef on. You can't run cattle here if it costs more than a hundred dollars for the home to carry a cow on. It's the price of cattle that has to pay for those fancy layouts."

He rubbed his bald head and picked up a hoof. "Do you know that son of mine defended the dudes?"

When the horse didn't even whinny, Pete let out his frustration with a blast of curse words that rebounded from the barn's tin roof and echoed in his own ears.

He was still bent over his horse's hoof when he heard a familiar call, "Hello, you withered old prune."

"Hey, Ben, I didn't hear you come up. I must be losing my hearing."

"Naw, you ain't," his neighbor answered with a laugh as he dismounted. "You was yellin' and cussin' so loud it's a wonder you heard me at all."

Pete tossed a couple of #6 nails into the crease of

217

his Stetson and straightened. "Where are you going so damn dressed up this early?"

Ben swept off his cowboy hat and made a low bow. "I rode five miles in my best striped gambler's pants to have the great pleasure of tellin' you goodbye."

Pete dropped the shoeing hammer. "Where you headed?"

"Me an' my town widow is takin' off today for California."

"Why California?"

"That's where my other gal is."

"Can't you make a choice?"

"Hell yes." Ben chuckled. "I figure a man of my ability sort of owes it to the ladies to spread hisself around."

"You long-nosed rascal. I hope that town widow tears you limb from limb."

Ben stood at stiff attention beside his mount. "She won't. She likes me intact."

"And I'd give anything to see you pussy-whipped. How long a vacation is this?"

Ben rolled his hat brim, lowered his voice and in a stage whisper mouthed the words, "I'm retirin'."

Pete snorted. "In all the time I've known you, you've never stayed away from that buzzard's roost you call a ranch for more than a week."

Ben grinned. "Arizona may call me back someday. I was borned on this river." His eyes swept the horizon, as he took a deep breath. "The smell of this desert is stronger to me than rabbit scent to a coyote." Lowering his voice, he added, "I'm leavin', though. For good."

"I don't believe it."

"Shee-ut. I knew you wouldn't." Reaching into his pocket, Ben said, "That's why I brought this certified check from Gladys Luscomb to show you."

Pete swallowed hard.

Ben stuck his face close to his neighbor's. "I toldja two years ago I expected to get my hands on that red-head and her money. I teased her up but never did get a satisfyin' hold on her." He waved the check. "I sure as hell talked her out of a big hunk of dough."

"What have you got on her?"

"Nothin', you old fool. I sold her my ranch."

Pete grabbed the check. "Fifty-five thousand dollars! You robbed her."

"She knows it." Ben laughed. "But like Elwin says, 'If you want something, buy it. It's worth it.'"

"That dude husband of hers would."

Seconds ticked by. Pete handed back the check. Each horse raised up a hind leg and stamped to discourage flies.

Ben shuffled his boots in the soft dirt. "There's some more news you'll be interested in hearin'. Elwin says he's goin' back to lawyerin' more and cowboyin' less."

"Hooray!"

"Don't look for him to be outa your hair altogether. He'll be spendin' weekends now and then."

Pete slumped against the post. "The Old Johnson Place they bought along with your outfit makes the Luscombs' holdings bigger than mine."

Ben pocketed the check and patted his shirt front. "You asked me when I thought they was gonna quit cowboyin' an' leave. Answer is, they ain't never gonna leave. Fact is, they're expandin'. I heard about plans comin' to a head over there that you don't know nothin' about."

Pete leaned against his horse, looked up and searched the wide and silent expanse of cloudless sky. "We need rain."

Ben swung into his saddle. "You don't know the best yet."

"Spill it all."

"Nope. That's enough. I've told you over half of what you know already."

Pete whirled and smacked the post with his palm. "Why, you...you...."

"Yeah," said Ben spitting off the left side of his horse, "you've forgot more'n I'll ever learn. Just because I only got a third-grade education don't make me so dumb I can't see that ranchers has got to catch up to what's happenin'. There's only so much land, and we're goin' to get more than dudes movin' in on us—hunters, fishermen, hikers, campers—hell, Pete, you know the government is only leasin' you *grazin' rights* for most of your operation. Fred wised up. How I'd like to see your face when he—"

"When Fred what?" Pete said, cutting his neighbor short. He sensed the statement forming in Ben's mind, and he wasn't ready to hear it, especially from Ben's taunting lips.

He was relieved when Ben shook his head, waggled his fingers and said, "I ain't tellin'. However, to get back to the ranch sale, I figure I more'n got even with Gladys for not lettin' me cuddle her up. I sold her six of her own yearlin's I branded for myself." He winked. "Mavericks, of course."

Staring open-mouthed, Pete listened to his neighbor's whistle, watched him spur his horse's right shoulder and make a showoff turn as he called, "When you get fed up with the way you're livin', sell out an' follar me. Ya *hoo*." In a clatter of hoofs he was off down the road.

Pete watched until Buzzard Ben was out of sight. With a sigh, he bent over and picked up his horse's left hind foot and inspected the underside. He realized he wasn't going to get rid of the Easterners any more than he going to get rid of brush that popped up and choked out grass. He could only dig his boot heels in the ground and slow things down a little.

The horse jerked his hind leg and whinnied.

"Whoa, boy." Pete admitted to himself he'd worried for a long time Fred and Lita might get married; now he owned up to the fact. He sighed and mumbled, "Whenever you get a male and a female together at the right time and right place...I know this: a man can't fight it. I put off marrying longer than Fred, but I got caught. Only safety a man has is distance, and it's tough for him to stay away forever. Even bulls that have been dry-codding it and running together during the winter, beat it out of the hills in the early spring and fight each other for the privilege of serving the cows and heifers."

When the tied animal jerked its leg, Pete yelled, "Whoa. Quit kicking. I'm not hurting you, and your feet need protecting."

There came a steady clink-clink of metal, as Pete moved to the front feet, removed old shoes, and, after trimming and rasping hoofs, fitted and hammered new shoes into place.

"You know, Dunny, it's a damn good thing a man can't see what's coming in life. Hell, he chases tail without the least idea what he's letting himself in for. When he gets what he wants, he winds up with one whole hell of a lot more than he bargained for. And what's more, God Almighty sure knew what he was doing when he gave us a life of three score and ten. Living too long is just asking a man to put up with too much change. When I think what Pappy would do about dudes—but hell, he'd use a shootin' iron. Me? I put up with them, and my son is going to marry one."

The old cowman dropped a hoof and stepped back while the horse pawed the dry, cracked earth. Toeing his box of tools along the ground, he lifted the hoof again. "As for progress, all a cow puncher wants to do is take it easy, improve little by little. A damn dude roars in and kicks up more dust than a wild West bronco in a rodeo stampede."

After a few more taps with the hammer, he dropped the clincher bar and hitched up Levi's, chaps and underdrawers that were sliding down over his bony hips. "Those sons-in-law of mine are going to razz hell out me—especially the Bible-thumping one. He'll lecture me on how overgrazing went on before Jesus was born and accuse me and other ranchers of abusing the land. Dunny, we are not doing any such damn thing. We are starting to fence the range so we can take care of it—improve it."

Carrying the box of tools into the shed, he kicked himself mentally. *Hell, what's the matter with me? Everything is turning out the way I planned. Our place and the Old Johnson Place, plus Ben's, will be one unit. Fred will have a great outfit to run. Pearl and I have our home here....* After a pause, he mused, "Pearl has probably known all along how this would turn out. So what's my problem?"

Pete picked up his Stetson and slapped it against his chaps before putting it on. He took a curry comb off a hook and began long, sweeping strokes along the length of the horse's back. Grayed-brown hairs and dander mingled and rose in warming summer air.

"Dunny, I know why I've been such a sore ass. *I* wanted to buy the Old Johnson Place and turn it over to Fred. It galls me that Elwin got the job done." He leaned into the curry comb. "It galls the *hell* out of me."

He pronounced the Luscombs' names with three long syllables, "El-ll-win, Gl-ad-us, Ll-ee-ta," and thought about the coming of the dudes. Reminded, he relived shared experiences. His touch with the currycomb grew lighter, and strokes lengthened on the horse's back.

Looking across the river, he tipped his hat. "I have to give you Easterners credit. You try. You're not deadheads either." He hung up the comb and rubbed the animal's back with his bare hands. "Dunny, when it comes right down to it, I like those dudes. Actually, after two years, they're not outsiders anymore."

Pete buckled on spurs, his thoughts racing. *I'm going to ride over to Luscombs' Wickiup and shake hands. We can discuss things now we're caught in the same loop and will be working the same herd. I wonder if they'll mention the wedding.* He licked his upper lip, bit his lower, and shouted, "Wedding!" *Will the ceremony be Eastern formal?*

"By grab," he mumbled, "I'll watch my gosh darned language, but I won't wear a 'monkey' suit."

Reaching overhead for a hair pad and blanket, he whispered in his horse's ear, "Dunny, I'll bet some folks are going to say my son stuck his dick in the cash register." He chuckled. "You want Indian, Elwin? Fine. We'll put some authentic Apache blood in your grandkids' veins."

He swung the saddle onto the horse's back, settled it and reached down for the front cinch. His chuckling stopped abruptly.

Grandkids? Oh, my God! They'll be my grandkids, too. Fred's been badgering me to make cattle our cattle tougher by crossing Eastern Braymers and

Western Herefords. I didn't know his first test might be crossbreeding our East and West families.

Pete's laughter boomed louder than the answering horse's whinny. "Hell, Dunny, I'll build a loop big enough to hold us all."

The old cowboy worked the latigo through the cinch and rigging rings to hold the saddle in position. As he pulled on the wraps, he sang out, "Hang up my spurs? Not me! Our grandkids will need help getting started."

He buckled the flank cinch and stamped his boot heels till the spur rowels jingled. "Damn, I haven't felt this good in years."

THE END